On the Run

This story is dedicated to my mother and to all refugees, immigrants and especially their children originating from the lost German native lands Silesia, Pommerania and East Prussia.

My special thanks are reserved for Sir Edward C. Eates, my English friend, who advised me on the wording of the English manuscript.

JEAN-CHRISTIAN DE MONS

ON THE RUN

Childhood memories from 1944 to 1955

The narrative writer was born in the lost German "Far East" in the midst of war and confusion, not the best time to grow up. In his autobiography he takes us through difficult times and different places and shows us the kind of impediments that had to be mastered every day ... unbelievable in our orderly times.

Bibliographical information of Deutsche Nationalbibliothek
[the German National Library]
Deutsche Nationalbibliothek [the German National Library] has registered this publication in the German National Bibliography. Detailed bibliographical data may be found online at http: //dnb.dnb.de.

Coverdesign, Layout, produced and published by
BoD – Books on Demand, Norderstedt, Germany
ISBN: 978-3-7528-7478-5

Inhalt

Chapter 1

On the Run

Before reaching our final destination, a small village in Lower Saxony, a German province in Northwestern Germany, our trip began in January 1945 in chilling frost and deepest snow. But before I tell you all that happened then, let me begin with myself.

It was 1941 when I was launched into this cruel world. It happened to be in the commercial, administrative and cultural hub of the Prussian province Silesia and former member of the Hanseatic League, the city of Breslau (called Wroclaw now).

My elder brother Wolf could still remember my father, who was an army officer in the reserve and was killed in action as captain of the infantry at the Eastern front. I, however, appeared just three months after his death, a result of his last leave from duty in France. It seems to be strange that he was a lecturer at the philosophical and theological faculty of the university in Breslau and at the same time Lutheran pastor in a small community south of the city.

My mother belonged to one of the oldest Silesian clans of the landed aristocracy. After my father's death she continued to handle the administrative functions of the parish until a friend of my father, the only remaining "shepherd" and catholic priest, took over this job. My mother could keep the official residence but stayed most of the time at the manor of her parents near Oels, east of Breslau.

What is it that a small boy aged just three years remembers of the earliest days of his conscious existence?... The light and friendly kids room with its white crib and my greatest treasure, a small mouth organ. One day it slipped from my hand and down on the top of the awning in front of the main entrance. I was unable to explain this "catastrophe" to anybody and was very sad, but finally I forgot it. Among my wooden toys was a beautiful fortified castle with painted pewter figures of knights and horses that I got from my grandfather. There was also my beloved sawdust-filled white rabbit and cuddle companion named "Hopsi" that was dragged around everywhere.

Our chicken pen was situated above the separate garage and could be reached by wooden stairs. Every morning my mother used to collect the still warm eggs from the nests.

In the wintertime my playmates and I enjoyed staying in the warm cowsheds and horse stables of our neighbors and watching the farmhands milking the cows and carrying out the manure, or we played in the hayloft above the stables.

On the even sandy place situated in front of our protestant church the older children were playing with glass marbles and skipping-ropes. Games like "Himmel und Erde" (Heaven and Earth) were also popular.

At the Eastern fringe of the village there was a railway line with barriers and a small station. Frequently endless cargo trains with military vehicles and other equipment were passing, pulled by noisy steam locomotives. My brother loved to place coins on the tracks and retrieve them after a heavy train had passed over and flattened them. He also used to lie down on the black ballast of the railway embankment and press his ears onto the tracks to listen if a train was approaching.

He loved to annoy me by stuffing caterpillars, bugs, earthworms and similar delicacies into my mouth and was extremely satisfied when I spat them out with disgust or swallowed them by mistake.

I, too, remember the many horse- and oxen-drawn carriages and the sledges in winter carrying cargo and loads of trunks.

My grandfather, where we used to live later when my mother

became a widow, owned a black-and-white checkered German dog called "Thieras" that licked my face continuously when I was playing outside. Thieras was a perfect bodyguard and was ready to attack strangers who dared to come too close to me. Both Thieras and our small dachshund "Zumper" loved to chase together hares, pheasants and crows.

Hanging over the large oval table in the dining room was a huge brass candelabra. For many years a team of swallows used to build its nest there. When we were sitting at the table for a meal, these birds entered and left regularly and undisturbed through the upper part of one window that was kept open for them, to move unmolested and to feed their young ones. From time to time they dropped their "name card". There was a huge brass plate positioned underneath to avoid spoiling the white table cover.

The last Christmas was celebrated in the vast drawing room in Briese Castle, which belonged to my grandfather's family. It was adorned with large impressive paintings, and one of them reappeared recently in the Museum of Art in Los Angeles.

In the fireside were burning huge oak logs. The traditional Christmas tree, however, was too large and always erected in the spacious central hall underneath the belfry that adorned the impressive baroque building. The fir tree was so high that the old butler had to climb up the standing ladder to light or extinguish the wax candles. The lower branches were decorated with "Lebkuchen" (gingerbread), sweets and cookies for us children. On New Year's morning we were permitted to strip the tree.

Suddenly a few days later army staff and civilians came swarming into the castle and we returned home to prepare the flight to the West. Meanwhile my grandmother prepared a trek with horse-drawn carriages and arranged a meeting point with my mother.

The parsonage resembled a beehive. Relatives and refugees from regions already in the hands of the Red Army had found a temporary shelter at our home. Even the chicken pen and the empty garage served as accommodation. The evacuation order of the NS authorities was given only when Breslau became the target of the Russian artillery. As a wise precaution our mother had already long before started to send parcels with garments by mail to the West, but unfortunately all the trouble had been in vain; everything was somehow lost and never arrived at its destination.

Our agreed-upon meeting with the trek failed, because the phone and telegraph service to the East did not work anymore. We had the incredible luck to join a farmer, who left with an old-fashioned wedding coach, the last means of transport in the village. He dropped us at a railway station further west that was still in operation. Mum was carrying a rucksack and a shoulder bag; my brother had a back sack too and a small suitcase, which contained some documents and valuables, but that was stolen while he was in a state of exhaustion and neglected vigilance at Dresden railway station later on. I was just carrying a shoulder bag and had to hold the leash of our dachshund Zumper. We caught an absolutely overcrowded passenger train, probably the last one. The doors were blocked by luggage and masses of people. A few decent fellow travelers pulled us inside one carriage through a window. We boys and our dog found place on top of the hand luggage of the racks. The smell of sweat, urine and tobacco fumes was overwhelming but it was warm contrary to the glacial temperatures outside. The trip lasting several days was often interrupted by interminable stops on sidetracks somewhere due to repair works or in order to let troop carriers and supply trains of the Wehrmacht (armed forces) pass by. At Bischofswerda, an important railway junction further west, were the first signs of bombings on railway installations and rolling stock. The tracks were destroyed or blocked, and repair works and clearing activities were underway. Our train could not pass at this time, so we left it and walked through the wreckage to the other side of the station, where another passenger train was just about to be assembled. In spite of the confusion, Red Cross staff were tending the injured, auxiliary staff was distributing "Ersatzkaffee" (substitute coffee) and hot soup from a field kitchen.

After additional interminable stops and impediments we finally reached Dresden at nighttime. As a precaution it was in complete darkness but had not suffered any bombings yet. It had been spared by the Allied bombing commands, because it did not have strategic value and had no industry of war importance. The concentrated and devastating bombing happened later, when we were already again on the move. As there happened to be no more connection further West for a couple of days, we were directed to a giant underground air-raid shelter near the central railway station, where we slept on straw but got heavy woolen army blankets for cover. The noise was incredible, especially from the crying kids and babies, but soon we fell into an exhausted leaden sleep. The following night we were extremely lucky to catch an unannounced train further on. As we could not find a way to get in and mum was already in despair, a compassionate member of the postal staff slipped us into the parcel and mailbox carriage of the train going to Leipzig. We were squeezed between the piled-up mail sacks bearing the symbols of an eagle and the swastika.

On this route we experienced our first attack of fighter planes on our train. When the train stopped, people left the carriages in panic and crept underneath the train or took shelter in ditches and behind trees. The locomotive was not hit and there was no serious damage. The planes did not return, so we continued our trip using diversions and waiting endlessly on side tracks of marshalling yards until we finally reached the burning and smoke-covered city of Leipzig, which had just been the target of an air raid. Again we found protection in an air-shelter crammed with people. This time we were unable to sleep because of the moans of the countless injured victims of the recent bomb attack and the crying of those who had given up hope.

After a long wait and listening to the rumors we were informed about a train leaving soon for Halle, an industrial city further in the northwestern direction. When we arrived there we were again confronted with fire, smoke and destruction. After we had been treated again with “Ersatzkaffee” and hot soup we were directed to the improvised Red Cross station for the delousing procedure a result of the impossible hygienic situation of the refugees and homeless at this time of the war. After having received our stamped documents that we were free of lice and contagious diseases we were released and wandered through the ruined city in search of the home of the brother of my grandmother (my father’s side), Professor “Ohm” W. S. It was a miracle: the house situated in the suburbs of Halle was unscathed and in perfect condition. Uncle Walther and his wife were of course very surprised to see us alive. There we embraced also “Machen” my grandmother, who had managed to leave her residence in Breslau much earlier together with her youngest daughter, and was just about to leave for the West. There we got news about the general situation and about the whereabouts of relatives who had managed to keep contact. We were very happy to hear that “Hitta”, our other grandmother, had finally reached her brother with her trek after many adventures.

The hospitable professor and his wife even started a fire in the hot water boiler, and thanks to the still-operating water supply in this suburb, we could enjoy the indescribable extravagance of an intensive bath with good soap and decent towels. Finally after such a long time the three of us and our pitiable dachshund, who had been absolutely famished, got something substantial to eat. After our laundry had been done and dried and a wonderful sleep in beds covered with white linen, we started for our last stage towards Magdeburg. This train was again a target for Allied fighter planes. This time, however, we had a lot of casualties and some passengers were killed by guns.

The corpses were left behind. The personal documents alone

were collected for the authorities. The situation was not favorable for a burial on the spot as the ground was frozen hard as stone. From the train we could observe a bombing fleet flying in the direction of Berlin and returning later after having disposed of its deathly cargo, and some engaged in air battles and were hit, burning or trailing black smoke behind them, crashing and exploding.

It was in Magdeburg where we experienced something ghostly. Explanations were given to me later on like many others for facts and happenings that I did not yet understand being just a small kid. The city had just suffered an air raid where devilishly devised incendiary phosphor bombs had been dropped. We saw victims burning like torches running in panic through the rubble, turning about on the cobble stones and jumping into the round firefighting water storages trying to get rid of their burning garments. As soon as they got out of the water the fire started again. I will never forget the sweet smell of burned human flesh and the charred black remains of human beings scattered everywhere. In spite of the chaos the rail transport still worked somehow. From an improvised small station some way outside of the city we caught a local train and, unmolested by air attacks, reached Haldensleben, a small industrial city at the "Mittellandkanal" (Midland Canal).

It was pure luck! We were alive and not injured! Our suitcase with documents and valuables was gone, but our faithful companion Zumper the dachshund was still with us. Always, when the situation got critical, we put him into my brother's rucksack and you could see just his head peering out. Our little bodyguard survived the following years. We walked the last 8 km to Bodendorf, the landholding of Count v.d. S. the elder brother of my grandmother (my mother's side), who was born there.

When we arrived, Gisela, my mother's unmarried younger sister, was busy killing a chicken in front of the kitchen house. She was so surprised that she dropped the axe onto the chopping block. The already decapitated chicken escaped, steered by reflexes, in the direction of the park, where it finally fell quivering onto the snow. She had abandoned all hope and considered us already lost.

My grandmother's sister-in-law was a born von R., a relative of the famous fighter pilot of World War I, "The Red Baron". She was nicknamed Auntie "Peppo" and was a rather authoritarian personality. She was unable to understand the situation of the uprooted refugees, who had lost everything until the moment, when she herself had to give up everything. We were considered parasites and were not invited to live in the spacy manor. We were staying in the garret of the kitchen house, and the long room was divided for us by a thick curtain fixed on a clothes line. The habitant on the other side was a bombed-out lady from Berlin. Mrs. Boettcher was a born Englishwoman and wife of a German general, who had been taken as a POW by the Americans. Their only son had been killed in action during the Allied invasion in France. She was one of the countless human beings we met during our odyssey whose life had been completely turned upside down by the war. She was a distinguished and cultured personality and always impeccable in her appearance even while working in the kitchen and in the garden. She and my grandmother got on very well with each other and they became lifelong friends.

Hitta my grandmother was of course living in the manor. She had a cozy little room in the attic that was heated by a small barrel-like furnace. There were continuous disputes about something or the other between Hitta and Peppo; they had extremely differing characters. Hitta's brother, Uncle Pitz, joined the Nazi's for a simple reason. They had introduced some very clever laws supporting agriculture and especially large land holdings that were perfect for rational production. Even shortly before surrender he was very active organizing a last resistance, erecting anti-tank barriers and traps and in training youngsters at the anti-tank weapons (bazookas). The radio news of the "hero's death" of his beloved leader was a great shock for him. When you take into consideration that his cousin was the former German ambassador in Moscow until 41 and was hanged by the Nazis for being a member of the resistance group, which nearly managed to kill Hitler, such an attitude seems to be inconceivable.

Even in the provincial hamlet Bodendorf we were confronted continuously with the events of war. From time to time the fields and forests were hit by stray bombs dropped by planes in distress, wanting to get rid of their heavy and dangerous cargo. In the trees of the forests you found silvery "lametta" (strips of aluminum foil) dropped by the Allies to confuse the German defense radar equipment. At midnight we could observe from our attic window the faraway reflections in the sky of the burning cities.

It was amazing that the postal service was still working. We got mail from relatives in the West, but it took a long time to reach us.

One evening, after darkness had set in, a friend of Auntie Gisela from her schooldays slipped stealthily into the kitchen house. He was in the uniform of an infantry man and confided in us that he was a deserter. That signified death sentence when they got him. Gisela organized some civil garments for him and he stayed the whole following day hidden in the attic. In the night he left unseen as he had come. Much later we got the message that he had slipped through and had reached his Southern Bavarian destination unharmed.

Shortly before the end of the war deserters appeared more frequently at our place and asked for help. We sent them to a field barn where they could sleep unmolested in the hay. There was a rumor that German soldiers had shot the guards of an army depot when they refused to open the gates. According to another rumor, undernourished corpses with striped garments were found in a forest, victims of a death march of concentration camp inmates. People talked about raids and holdups by foreign workers from the bombed industries over whom the authorities had lost control.

Ignoring the uncertain situation my granduncle took care that the fields were cultivated properly. The mostly foreign farmhands and workers stayed on, because they were extremely frightened of the Russians and were happy that they had got a roof over their heads and their daily provision.

One day in May, when nature had already started to bloom, we were surprised by the unusual silence. There were no more detonations, no more antiaircraft guns to hear. The bombing fleets and German army vehicles and tanks had disappeared from the streets. Suddenly a single jeep with a white star on its bonnet approached from the thoroughfare with an officer and a black driver. It was the first time I was confronted by a man of dark skin. I was just playing in the front yard and was the first to welcome the foreign military guests, and directed them to the kitchen house. In the meantime a convoy with trucks, jeeps and light armored cars had appeared. They were ranged orderly in a row, guards were ordered to different positions and a search party was sent out.

Meanwhile, Uncle Pitz appeared on his riding horse, posing as "Herrenmensch" (masterful man) to negotiate with the commander of the unit. The result was that the count and his family could remain in the manor, but they had to retreat to the servants' quarters in the attic and the chapel. The rest of the building was transformed into a commanding center of the US Army. A radio-communication truck took position in the center of the park and a couple of tents were erected. All rooms were searched and suspicious appearing documents and items as well as the hunting rifles were confiscated. A few other valuable items disappeared, but the greatest loss was a historical scimitar from a glass cabinet, which is probably hanging now at the wall of the living room of a war veteran somewhere in the United States

… "spoils of war". An ancestor, Field Marshal Matthias Count v.d. S., was appointed commander in chief of the Venetian land forces. On one occasion he was presented with the personal jewel-studded scimitar by his adversary the Osman Pasha and commander of a fleet in esteem for his strategic genius during a conflict on the island of Corfu at the beginning of the 18th century.

A lively activity now started around the estate. The cook took over the command in the kitchen and "victory cakes" were prepared on the day of armistice, and my brother and I were treated to a slice. I did have a very good understanding with the commander's driver, Sergeant Charlie. He slipped chocolate and chewing gum into my pocket and taught me some English words and phrases.

One day the "Amis" (Americans) ordered some workers of the estate to dig a huge pit beside the kitchen house. Some trucks arrived later on and disposed of there the supply goods of a nearby dissolved German forces depot. Everything was sprinkled with petrol and fire was set to the whole lot. When the people had disappeared my brother and some other village boys retrieved some tinned food with the help of hooked poles. When everything was ashes the pit was filled up again.

Shortly after, our American occupation force left for Berlin.

After a few quiet days a small unit of French forces appeared and accepted the hospitality of the count just for a short period. This time, however, any problems of understanding did not exist; all grown-up members of the family spoke French. For the officers even some bottles of hidden French red wine were sacrificed during a frugal dinner.

When the representatives of "La Grande Nation" had left, the estate became a communication center of the British Forces. They remained for a longer time. Again a radio truck was parked in the middle of the park. That temporary regional headquarter became rather busy. There was a continuous coming and going.

Opposite the small lake the pastures were flattened with rollers in order to prepare a landing strip. A small hut was erected and the landing strip was marked with a couple of heavy red-and-white-painted oil barrels at both sides. Later, three small, single-engine planes arrived and were parked beside the hut with the wind sleeve. The camouflaged planes were used for messenger services. One of the young pilots was on good terms with Mrs. B., the Englishwoman. In spite of the order for all Allied forces that forbade friendly contacts with the Germans he enjoyed conversing with us. Our mother grasped this opportunity to practice some English. In 1935 she was supposed to stay with English relatives in Hampstead/London to learn English; her marriage, however, made that impossible. There were countless interesting subjects to talk about. One fine summer day the pilot broke all rules and took me for a flight over the area. For me it was a unique and unforgettable event. Who would have guessed at this time that much later in life planes would be my working place? At last also the British Army got their moving order for Berlin.

After a couple of days, when displaced persons were roaming the area we heard one evening the strange song of a unit of the "Red Army" approaching with horse-drawn wagons from the east. The marching song sounded like "O lalapot ... lalapot ...!" The melody is still in my ears. They left the district road and took over the village and estate. Without discussion the whole family was thrown out of the manor: "You capitalist ... out!" Uncle Pitz reacted immediately. He had heard gruesome stories about the Russians who had shot owners of large landed property on the spot and violated the women and often killed them afterward. That did not happen here. The Russian commander, who spoke some broken German, took care that law and order was maintained by his soldiers; he had to overlook, however, plundering and the consumption of alcohol, so as not to lose the loyalty of his Mongolian combat troops. Everything that had some kind of attraction or was useful was piled on their "Panje" wagons. Women had to deliver jewelry so far they were so naive still to carry it. Especially in demand were watches. I can still hear the shouting of the pilfering Mongol, who searched our attic room: "Uri, uri!" pushing aside everything blocking his way with the butt of his rifle. He was wearing already a couple of watches on his arm and a couple of pocket watches in his uniform jacket. Later, when I had lost my fear of these wild men and had closer contact with one of these child-loving Mongols, he often put one of his pocket watches to my ear that I could listen to the ticking of the works. When he was displeased about something he shouted, "Nix gut, dawai, dawai!" There was a steady demand for alcohol, because the supply of vodka was strictly rationed. Considering this situation Uncle Pitz' in cold panic had secretly sunk some barrels with industrial spirit in the lake. As they were not sufficiently charged, they appeared again, floating on the surface, barely visible in the water. By chance they were discovered by some "red armists" who were enjoying a boat trip. Barrel by barrel, each was fished from the lake. Subsequently all doors and windows had to be barred to protect the village and surroundings from the drunken hordes. Fortunately the captain had collected all the arms and locked them in the safe room of the manor. But even he could not prevent some beatings and rapes in the village. Everybody made three crosses when the men were sober again, but even many days afterward you could see the soldiers' inflamed lips, faces and eyes caused by the high-percentage spirit unfit for human consumption. When they were sober, they were good-natured, easygoing and helpful.

The chief of the field kitchen missing his faraway family had taken a fancy to me. I was his "Germanski maltschik" (German boy). He secretly supplied me with leftover "chleb" (bread), which he stuffed into my shirt, and ordered me in broken German that I should appear daily equipped with a tankard right after the distribution of food to his fellow Mongols. It was filled with his ladle to the brim with soup and pieces of meat. So he helped us to overcome our provision problems for a while. Meat was nonexistent at this time and we were normally living like vegetarians.

Very romantic was the nightly campfire in the park where we curious brothers were permitted to join the troop. To the melodies of a balalaika and an accordion the men were dancing in groups encouraged by the rhythmic shouts and clapping hands of the circle of onlookers. At such occasions vodka and "papirossi" (Russian cigarettes) were thrust on us and they slapped their thighs and doubled up with laughter when we had a fit of coughing and red faces while nearly asphyxiating. They also let us ride on their shaggy small "Panje" horses. For us boys even this distracting time came to an end. The unit was ordered to take quarters in the barracks of Haldensleben and the family could move out of the kitchen house and back into the stripped manor.

Shortly after, a terrible accident occurred. Another uncle from Silesia, Erich v. K., survived the war completely intact. After having been released very early from the British POW camp he joined us. With a battered wood gas–operated lorry he had started a local transport business. One day, when repairing a damage stretched out underneath, a reckless driver of a heavy troop carrier drove over his lower legs. He had to undergo an immediate amputation. He was forced to spend the rest of his life in a wheelchair. Much later, living near Munich he was, however, able to work and to drive a small car specially constructed for invalids.

The communists had taken over the administration in the Soviet-occupied zone, after having been persecuted in the time of the Nazis. In our area at first it created a chaos. In our village a "red" mayor and the schoolmaster had taken over the command. My brother was obliged to go to school regularly from now on. After having had a free life since the end of 1944, he like other pupils, especially those without a father, did not enjoy it at all. The teacher had a hard time and was furious, because my brother was continuously causing trouble, was disrespectful, rebellious and made imprudent remarks. For this very reason he was often disciplined, being slapped and treated with the stick in front of his schoolmates. Uncle Pitz seeing the problems took over the role of the missing father and punished my brother on several occasions with his riding whip, which helped, however, only temporarily.

At harvest time the whole population was ordered to help, because there were only a few horses left and the still existing mechanical equipment could not be used for lack of petrol. Because of the critical food situation the grain, sugar beet and potato crop was strictly controlled to guarantee that everything was delivered to the authorities. Still, the population managed to hoard foodstuff and to slaughter secretly "black". In the later course of events the estate was appropriated by the communist authorities, and my granduncle and his family had no other choice but to leave just with little carry-on luggage for Bavaria. As soon as they were gone, the population looted the manor and took away all the heavy furniture and everything else the Mongols had not taken. In the storage compartment of the attic hidden underneath a pile of junk they found some boxes of hard-cured sausages hidden and completely forgotten. However, they got so spoiled by mold that they were unfit for human consumption.

We refugees with bourgeois names were inconspicuous and were allowed to stay on in the kitchen house, but we had to pay a small rent to the authorities as the estate was now people's public property.

The following winter was extremely cold in Germany, but living in the countryside we did not die of hunger like many people in the big cities. In summer and autumn we had been very busy collecting edible provisions. For days we got just "Heaven and Earth" (apple puree and potatoes) or hulled grain with cooked dried apple slices.

The small lake became covered with ice and we enjoyed ourselves sliding on its frozen surface. My daring brother wanted to find out if the thinner ice at a certain place was solid enough and promptly broke through. In my childish ingenuousness I wanted to rescue him. Running towards him I slipped and fell backwards, hitting the ice with the back of my head. My mother who had heard my brother shouting for help and seeing him thrashing in the ever-growing hole in the ice fetched a ladder and pushed it to the opening and pulled my brother Wolf onto firmer ice. The consequence was that he caught pneumonia, but that was cured soon. I however suffered a longer-lasting problem. On the same evening, when I squatted on my chamber pot I told my mother, "I can see two lamps!" As there was just one lamp bulb hanging from the ceiling, she presumed that something was not all right with me. The next day we walked through the high snow to the public hospital in Haldensleben for a medical checkup. After hours of waiting we were taken care of. After a thorough examination the specialist finally informed my mother that I had suffered a cerebral concussion and a disorder of the right optic nerve. He told us that I was in need of a pair of glasses immediately in order to correct my sight. Unfortunately there were none available at this time. My sight problem worsened and I began to squint and, in addition, to stammer, which weighed heavily on me in the coming years.

One day my mother walked alone to Haldensleben to provide us with some essential items. On her way back home she was assaulted by a Russian soldier, beaten down, raped and robbed of her belongings. Fortunately she recovered from the shock and did not suffer any consequences later on. When she reported the incident to the criminal investigation department of the local police, she was told that such occurrences were common and that there was no way to take action against the members of the Soviet armed forces. The members of the occupying Red Army were "tabu". Caught "in flagranti" delinquents received just mild admonitions and mock penalties.

After some interruption, the mail between the four occupation zones started to function again and mum had a lively correspondence with relatives, friends and acquaintances long thought lost. She received the most adventurous reports. My grandfather (my mother's stepfather) already believed dead had surfaced again, released by the Americans, and had joined my grandmother Hitta, who had found a warm reception and new quarters in the villa of generous relatives in Buedingen/Hesse state near Frankfurt/Main. "Fiete", my father's youngest sister, succeeded in getting a residence permit in Goettingen (British Zone) for herself and her mother where they shared an already overcrowded apartment with other refugees. She suggested that we leave the Soviet zone as soon as possible to join them.

The actual incident that forced us to make a fast decision was a fire. My brother had repeatedly pilfered matches from the kitchen. In the vicinity of an extended field barn he had, unobserved and alone, started a straw fire. Favored by a wind blowing in the direction of the barn and scattered loose straw on the ground the fire had gotten out of control and spread to the wooden construction. Wolf, unable to stop it, had run away in panic. The barn burned down and its stored grain and seed potatoes were destroyed. I still remember the smell and taste of the partly burned potatoes we, together with the villagers, collected from the ashes. My brother up to now deceived everybody and lied consistently even to our mother. The Russians suspected sabotage, and soon after, a Soviet civilian and a German criminal investigator arrived and interrogated the members of the community. The well-meaning communist mayor Trippler, who took pity on my destitute mother, gave her the confidential advice to better leave inconspicuously before my brother, the presumed culprit, was taken by the Russians. Mum gave my auntie in the West a coded prearranged signal by telegram; she even risked picking us up, and we left under the cover of darkness. We had stored our few belongings on a small wooden handcart and moved in a Southern direction toward the "Harz" mountains. Fiete had reconnoitered the route very well and so we made good progress. From time to time I was put on top of the handcart when my feet started to hurt and I could not keep pace with the others. It did not rain and the exodus progressed uneventfully. Some part of the way we were able to get into the box wagon of a train; another time the driver of a lorry gave us a lift on his empty loading platform. Overnight we slept somewhere in a barn. In the middle of a night we managed to slip through the still poorly guarded border near Heiligenstadt on the slopes of the mountains. We reported to the local authorities and were sent to a delousing station where we took a cold shower and got our health certificate. Next we were told to proceed further and to report at the refugee assembly camp in Friedland. When we arrived there we were treated with a hot soup and "Ersatzkaffee" as in the war, then we had to fill out piles of forms. Thanks to the assistance of my clever aunt we were able proceed by train to the nearby city of Goettingen. After 1.5 years of separation we could finally embrace our fragile grandmother. Our dachshund Zumper had also survived without harm but had slimmed down to his bones.

Where and how I spent my youth I am going to reveal in the next chapter.

Chapter 2

The Village

There we were, in Goettingen, the famous university city in the southern part of Lower Saxony state in the British occupation zone. It was at that period absolutely crammed with homeless people especially from the lost provinces in the extreme East and those in Czechoslovakia. My aunt was already registered at the university for studying law and could remain there together with my grandmother. In the town residence, to which they had been assigned to by the authorities, were living besides the landlady about twenty persons including us, some sleeping in turns on the floor. The spacious apartment resembled a beehive.

To prevent uneven burdens from the masses of refugees, the homeless and bombed-out people, they were gradually distributed to villages of the county and this was handled by the district magistrate. Thanks to the extraordinary organizational talent of my young aunt, who had formerly been secretary at the army general staff in Breslau, very soon we got a residence permit for a small place not too far away in the eastern direction of the town. From the point of view concerning alimentation that was the greatest problem in those postwar years, mum and we were in a slightly better position than in urban areas.

On foot and with little luggage we reached our new accommodation the parsonage of the protestant pastor E. S., who became later "Uncle Ernst" for us.

It was May 19, 1946.

We were allocated to the only remaining room situated at the Northern corner of the half-timbered building. There was no chimney and for this reason the room had never been heated. It smelled musty and the walls were partly covered with a fine layer of mildew. First we slept on straw sacks on the floor boards until the pastor arranged two simple beds for us. Before falling to sleep our feet were kept warm for a while with heated bricks wrapped in some thin fabric. Our mother prepared our meals on a tiny oven, a so-called "Hexe" (witch), she had got from a helpful soul. The stovepipe led through the upper section of the window, where the glass panel had been replaced by a piece of tin with a circular opening to fit the pipe. Firewood, twigs and pine cones to start the fire had to be collected from the surrounding forests. In the beginning we got mostly soup. All edible products of fields, forests and meadows went in our "pot-au-feu" (stew). The small cooking hearth served also as heater in the cold season.

The big parsonage building resembled a dove cot with its inhabitants: continuous coming and going of foreign workers, displaced persons, bombed-out people from cities and refugees occupied the house from cellar to attic. For a while even the woodshed and the garage served as improvised sleeping quarters. Some fellow lodgers spoke just some broken German with a heavy accent. They originated from Ukraine and Poland. There was also the widow of an army officer like my mother from our native land; her son, Erdmann, of my age; and her mother. Erdmann became my first playmate of this period. As an only child he was much pampered by his mother as far as the situation made it possible. Mrs. von G. was in the lucky position of having rescued a couple of valuables that she was able to exchange at the farmers and on the black market in the city for foodstuff, garments and other items of need.

I also struck up a friendship with a strange old man, Mr. Jakuschinsky. He was an artist, a woodcarver. I still have the figure of a sitting owl and our clan's coat of arms reminding me of this skillful old man.

Never minding wind and weather, he often took me for a walk. On our tour we used to pass the stone quarry and followed the path along the Eastern fringe of the forest where he had left and was adding continuously new fascinating carvings on stumps and trunks of beech trees and stone pines like elephants, heads of dogs, birds and figures from fairy tales.

Up behind the parsonage existed the only ruin of a totally destroyed house of the village caused by artillery fire or a stray bomb. The cellar, however, was still accessible. For us boys it was an interesting place to explore and to look for something useful.

The rural "thump and thud" toilet was a brick construction at the side of the cement-covered cesspool and the outhouse of the parsonage, where the laundry was done in a wash cradle and boiled in a huge copper cauldron.

Toilet rolls were unavailable; instead, a packet of square-cut pieces of paper from probably leftover editions of the *Völkische Beobachter* (*NS News*) or the *Kirchenblatt* (*Church Messenger*) hung on the wall from a wire.

The contents of the dung reservoir were regularly emptied at the appropriate seasons – late autumn and early spring – by means of a long pole with a tin bucket fixed at its end. Bucket by bucket was lifted from the opening and filled into a cistern-tank on a handcart. Several cart loads were necessary to provide the vegetable garden of the pastor's wife "Ilse", which was situated east of the village near the cemetery, with sufficient dung. Curious as I was and watching the procedure closely, I slipped on one of those occasions and fell into the cesspool. It took a lot of water to get rid of the perfume. For some time I was the target for a lot of jokes and instead of my usual nickname "squinting buck" I was called "smelling badger", but the adults called me "Brüderchen" (little brother), which I preferred of course.

The other side of the parsonage was surrounded by a marvelous orchard, berry bushes and a flower garden. There was an espalier with a tasty variety of pears at the southern wall of the building. The pastor knew obviously a lot about the care and pruning of fruit trees. At picking time I was often called to help him and to try his fruit. For the first time at Easter in 1947 our mother hid some eggs and homemade caramel sweets in this orchard and we had to search for them (it was an old German custom). In exchange for some cigarettes, still a kind of currency at this time, she had got some eggs from a farmer and had dyed them by means of onion parings and decorated them with borrowed colored pencils. The sweets, caramel bonbons, were a simple by-product when molasses were prepared. The shredded sugar beets were boiled then pressed and the filtered liquid was run into the huge polished copper cauldrons normally used for laundry. After endless boiling and continuous stirring with large wooden spoons and sticks the sugar liquid was finally reduced to a dark brown syrup. One had to be very careful not to get hurt by the spurting stuff. The syrup was used as breadspread or for baking Christmas cookies. The sweets were made by mixing cream with syrup, then spreading the mass on a baking tray and heating it again until it had the right consistence. The mass was cut with a knife into small cubes or rhombic pieces and filled into the usual tin containers when cold.

My first harmless erotic investigation I shared with a farmer's pretty daughter of my age underneath an elder bush in the meadow of the parsonage, where the laundry was hung for drying. The girl often provided me with the crusty end cuttings of the loaves that nobody wanted and with slices of smoked sausages from her parents' pantry. But soon competition happened to appear on the scene. Emily was the pretty daughter of the owner of a large estate in the East, who had, like us, escaped from the advancing Russians. Her husband, an army officer, was missing, and there was a slim chance that he had been taken prisoner.

She was young, attractive and full of spirit, was fed up with uncertain waiting and received frequently male visitors of the "haute volée" from the area, who supplied her with provisions and other essential items. Our mother, a broadminded and compassionate character soon became a good friend of this vivacious lady. Mrs. H. was living in an improvised hut near the end of the village. The flat roof was sealed with tarred paper. Later when she moved away we "inherited" this palace. In the hot summer Emily and I used to play nude in the meadow and especially in the creek that passed behind the hut. Together we built a dam to facilitate the catching of tadpoles and other aquatic animals.

Emily's mother was an unusually good-looking and self-assured woman. The unassuming and inexperienced village people had never met someone like her before. One day she appeared from the East, just accompanied by her daughter, with a team of thoroughbred horses harnessed to a fully loaded covered wagon with rubber tires, something rare at this time, and had rented the primitive hut. Gradually she exchanged the horses, the wagon, oriental carpets and other items of value with the farmers and on the black market in Goettingen. For this reason she could afford to stay at home and was not forced like my mother to work on the field or do another job. The extensive fenced garden and orchard kept her busy. Mrs. H. appealed to me. She always smelled so good of perfume and smoked exotic cigarettes with a carved holder that was made of ivory, she explained to me. We passed a very dry and hot summer and she did not mind walking just dressed in a one-piece swimming dress, sandals, straw hat and sunglasses, carrying a basket through the thoroughfare of the village to our grocer's shop "Lindau". She was followed of course by the whispered remarks and jealous glances of the archconservative female folk hidden behind the window curtains. Much later appeared a new devoted admirer, Mr. Ring, with his enormous American "street cruiser", a cabriolet. He was a good-looking clever "black-marketeer", who turned to shady interzone transactions after the currency reform had taken place. In the course of events, politicians in the East and the West were equally involved and cheated by him. My mother told me much later about it. The reputed German magazine "Der Spiegel" (*The Mirror*) published a long article about that scandal. Mrs. H., adventuress by nature, decided to join this fortune hunter. She declared her husband dead and was free again. They arranged a simple civil marriage. The registrar was the baker K., a follower of the "Witnesses of Jehova". The ceremony took place in his bakery. According to the circumstances it was a sensation for this small village. Everybody who could quit his work was present, either to hiss and boo at the happy couple or to clap hands and cheer them on when they took place in the open pink Buick together with Emily and left trailing dust behind them.

Decades later I recognized her in a luxury hotel near Frankfurt/Main, and we had a nice chat reviving old stories. She had long been separated from her second husband, who spent a long time in prison, and had married again, this time a retired colonel. I met Emily too; this time she was a representative and buyer of fashion garments in Hong Kong for a German departmental store.

Adjoining the flagstoned thoroughfare at the eastern exit of the village, where the snow plough was usually parked, was a place with an impressive lime tree. In the summertime underneath in its shadow was the resting place for the free roaming geese and ducks of some people living nearby. Our dachshund "Jockel" roaming around alone one day had started to chase the more interesting geese around, and had finally killed two of them in his "hunting fever". There was of course a lot of hue and cry. My mother paid for the damage and all involved including the culprit enjoyed a "roasted geese party"!

In the warm season this place became also the campsite of vagrants, tramps and gypsies. When the latter approached with their horse-drawn caravans, the poultry in the whole village was brought into safety and all doors and windows were locked tight.

In spite of all precautionary measures the dexterous members of the troop always contrived to pocket something. We children were always warned not to get too close to the strange people as they were supposed to kidnap little children. I considered this talk as ridiculous, because the young gypsy women were always carrying babies in their arms. They went from house to house with outstretched open hands begging until they got something. If they did not like what they got, it was thrown disdainfully down, they stamped their feet furiously on the ground and started to scream and to swear. Everybody gave something just to get rid of them. This unusual outbreak of temperament was an impressive sight for us. The women were brightly dressed and carried a couple of bangles at their arms and ankles, flashing rings in their ears and adornments at one side of the nose and around the neck. Nowadays that is nothing special anymore. This exotic fashion has especially been taken over by young women. The dark-skinned men caught our attention because of their many gold teeth and the gaps in their dentures. Their principal occupation was the mending of metal containers like pots, cauldrons, tankards, buckets and tubs. They also traded horses, which were still employed for transport and fieldwork.

Because of the rationing of fuel, tractors remained in the barns.

There were some operated by wood gas, but not in our village.

Some gypsy troops gave acrobatic or magic performances. I was very curious about the inside of their rolling living quarters and was surprised by their orderliness and tidiness. Later the gypsy men were often seen with old oversized American "petrol-guzzlers", which they had acquired from members of the US forces paid for with money they had received from the German government as compensation for their persecution in the time of the so called "millennium" of the NS regime.

Another service was rendered by the knife grinder, who took care of the villagers' cutlery. With his pedal-operated equipment he made the round of the village and had always enough work to do, especially the sharpening of butcher knives, axes and shears.

Shortly after the currency reform a closed lorry came at regular intervals to sell basic household articles like pots, brooms, buckets, dishes, cutlery and so on. The bigger articles were hanging at the sides – it was really a driving showcase. Everybody could see that production had started again.

An always welcome visitor was Mr. Resebeck, the metal collector and scrapyard owner. For years he came with a horse-drawn freight wagon that was equipped with automobile wheels until a truck took over. He made his presence known with the help of a handbell, shouting, "Old iron, copper, lead, aluminum …!" For everything he gave some coins depending on the weight; for us, always enough to buy a handful of sweets at the village store. We boys collected and stored scrap in advance. In the surrounding forests and abandoned stone quarries, which served as rubbish deposits in later years, we found enough metal especially corroded war equipment like bayonets, rifles, handguns, ammunition boxes, shell cases, steel helmets and civil items like buckets, disused farm equipment, gutter pipes, prams, bicycles etc.

Outside the village in a western direction near the forest was an area covered with blackthorn bushes. In its center was a giant bomb crater. We called it "Erdfalle" (earth trap). This place was strictly forbidden for us children, but that of course made it especially alluring. In 1946 an abandoned "Flak" (antiaircraft gun) was still positioned there, its four barrels directed to the sky. When you pulled a lever it slowly began to turn. The older boys used it as merry-go-round but soon the battery was empty. The next time we went there the monster was gone, probably taken away by the British forces now stationed in Goettingen.

But there was still plenty to do for our unrestricted activities. Everywhere in this area one found empty artillery shells scattered around and piles of live ammunition, grenades and military equipment. There we discovered wide parallel tracks where absolutely nothing grew. A very heavy tank or another armored tracked vehicle must have passed there shortly before the end of the war.

The refugee children were of course poorly dressed; everything was darned or patched. At first we were called "rabble", but that soon passed and the situation improved when the native villagers noticed that we were decent people and not parasites or dregs of society. Using old material she was given by the farmers, neighbors and the pastor, our mother prepared some simple garments for us. She did not have anything to offer on the black market or to the later-established exchange center. Old disused pullovers and sweaters were carefully taken apart and the good threads of wool were used to knit something else. Smaller holes were darned or covered with patches in the form of circles, hearts or four-foiled clover leaves. My thick woolen stockings were darned again and again, but those were just used in the cold season. In the summertime I walked around barefoot. I always inherited the outgrown oversized garment of my brother Wolf. Shoes were not available for a long time. My only pair was beyond repair. Instead our village cobbler prepared a pair of primitive slippers for me that I used for two winter seasons. They were sturdy boards cut to the shape of my feet. In the front was just a wide canvas strap cut from some military equipment and fixed with a couple of wide-headed studs at the side. From time to time they got loose and had to be hammered tight again. As there was no profiled rubber sole they were rather dangerous and one learned to walk very carefully when the ground became slippery. Rubber soles, leather, nails, ropes, glass panes and countless other commodities of daily use were extremely scarce and sometimes unavailable as long as the German industry was paralyzed and did not produce. Nowadays we manufacture too much and have big problems in disposing of all the used-up consumer goods. But let us return to my slippers ... for sliding on the frozen surface of the fire-brigade pond and on the frozen surface of the streets they were perfect as long as there was no small obstacle that made me stumble and fall. No wonder that I returned home frequently with cuts, grazes and bleeding knees. Finally I got the laced boots of an older playmate who had outgrown them. Using the fur of a rabbit my mother tailored a pretty cap for me to keep my head warm in wintertime. All the kids envied me for it. Before I got it, my mother used to wrap her worn woolen shawl around my head. She was wearing then her still-good-looking fur coat with fitting cap, the only precious object she managed to rescue from Silesia. I did not have gloves, an item that children always tend to loose. I put my hands in my pockets or in a fur muff to keep them warm. The year 1947 was a very harsh winter. It was so cold that one evening, returning from the cowshed of farmer W., I could not open my hand that I had closed around the wooden handle of the tankard with milk when I returned home. In spite of the biting pain I had not dared to open and change hands, frightened about spilling the precious milk.

At that period I was always feeling cold and I was happy after having been washed standing in a bucket to slip into the snug bed joining mum. The fur coat served as an additional cover. The pillow was filled with sawdust and was made like the blankets from old unpicked flour sacks and sewn together to fit the straw sacks; later we got a worn mattress filled with grassweed. From long use this mattress had the usual depression in its middle to comfortably fit our behinds. For good smell mum had collected some lavender, dried it and filled small bags with it that were suspended from the walls and placed in the chest where we kept our garments to deter moths.

At the beginning the refugees like us owned just what they wore, with four to five layers on their body and what they were able to carry in their luggage during the flight from the East. We had the good fortune to carry some additional items in our handcart when we came from Bodendorf, which we picked up later from our grandmother in Goettingen. There was a surplus of prams that had been used by the people as means of transport. At that time, everything was put to use and nothing was wasted! Even the wood ashes were used as anti-slip on the roads and outside stairs in winter, as fertilizer in the gardens, together with sand for cleaning pots and as a means to prepare primitive soap. Potato- and other peels were still used for soup or fed to the poultry and rabbits. Deformed rusty nails were hammered straight and pieces of wire served as hooks, hinges or were used to repair holes in the meshed wire doors of the rabbit hutches. The leather of old, torn shoes was kept and had many uses. The hinges of our rabbit-hutch doors later on were made of such a material. At the very beginning refugees even used empty cans and steel helmets as cooking utensils. The sturdy rippled containers for gas masks were utilized to store dried foodstuff like flour, leaves of peppermint, blackberries, balm mint and so on for tea. The practical army field–cutlery set, foldable spades, picks and bayonets were still employed for years to come. Uniforms were altered and dyed.

My grandmother living in Goettingen received later a modest widow's pension. My grandfather had been working in the provincial administration in Breslau. With that income she even financed the law studies of her youngest daughter. (Both sons were killed in action and the other daughter was married to a former submarine commander, who was my godfather.) My grandmother was living very frugally and avoided all unnecessary expenses. Her ideal example was the Prussian king and philosopher Frederic the Great. It went so far that she found an appropriate use for a big swastika flag of the former regime she had found in a pile of rags. It was used as a sheet on the foldable camp cot I was sleeping on, when we were staying over-night in the city.

When "good currency" was in circulation again you could suddenly buy long-missed goods without rationing cards at the provision merchant's. Loose articles like sugar, salt and flour were filled into brown paper bags and weighed on big scale balances or on old-fashioned balances with different round brass or iron weights. After having returned home from shopping grandma transferred the articles into proper containers, folded the still-useful bags, put them in a growing pile in the cupboard and returned them from time to time to the grateful shop owner. We did the same in our village. Supermarkets with their already-packed articles in standard sizes did not exist yet. They were introduced decades later.

While still in Silesia, my grandma had demonstrated her masterstroke of cleverness. The former regime had introduced a law that just a maximum of 1,000 Reichsmark (RM; former currency) was permitted to be withdrawn from an account during a certain period. She, who despised and distrusted the authorities, had with wise foresight spread the whole family savings over sixteen different savings books. The rule was not changed after the war. Even in the West the manager of the existing branch of the bank was perplexed when she presented one day the pile of sixteen savings books with different account numbers and asked to be paid out the high amount of money. To make it short, she got her way and received the unusual high amount of Reichsmarks. A rule is a rule! It was used right away for essential items before the ongoing inflation diminished its value further.

When she applied later for a widow's pension, the civil servant in charge was shaking his head very impressed and remarked jokingly, "You cannot be a refugee, your records are in an unusually perfect order!" Her daughter had managed to rescue the family documents at the very last moment from our home, where they had been stored while Breslau was bombed. Both women were ingenious in improvisation and solving problems and knew very well how to commission articles in demand. When the narrow-gauge railway that passed our place some kilometers away was operating again, my granny came frequently to our place, equipped with a rucksack, cotton bags and a basket, to exchange items and especially cigarettes with the farmers for foodstuff. In even the later and better years an old widow supplied her with fresh eggs and an occasional chicken already plucked and drawn for the soup. Soon grandma was known to the ticket collector of the small train and always got a friendly helping hand. Before the train reached its final destination at a sidetrack down the cargo yard of the city's railway station, it stopped at the rear of her living quarters, which saved her a long walk.

The thoroughfare of the village was paved from one end to the other with basalt cobble stones; the country road, however, was as usual asphalted but even years after the end of the war in an incredible bad condition, probably caused by heavy tanks. There were so many potholes that it was impossible to avoid them when riding on a bicycle later on. The side streets of the village, however, were simple dirt roads and changed into a yellowish quagmire, as the area mainly had argillaceous loamy clay soil. Damaged walls of the old-fashioned framework houses were as in medieval times still repaired with exactly this material. Names of areas near the village were based on it. Down the "Hengstberg" (stallion mountain) in the east, for example, was the "Rote Ufer" (red bank), a favorite place to grow sugar beet and grain. In hot summers this soil turned into concrete. The hilly upper region near the village on the other hand consisted of limestone and calcareous earth. This kind of stone was rather soft and disintegrated quickly. We often discovered shells and other petrified fossils in the stone slabs.

Notwithstanding the fact that the community's treasury was nearly empty, the "council of the elders" decided to do something to improve the situation and to fix the village streets. "Old Lindau", the community courier, and "Town Crier", equipped with text and handbell, were sent out to inform the citizens about the news. For some reasons, possibly missing teeth, he was unable to articulate clearly, so after the announcement the people, not having understood anything, asked each other in dialect, "What did he say again?" But after having studied the text they knew what was going on. The whole population that could move was requested to appear on a certain Saturday morning equipped with hammers and aprons at an indicated stretch of one of the village streets. The farmers with horse wagons were ordered to transport stones from one of the nearby stone quarries, and these were distributed on the flat rolled street. Kids and grandmothers including everybody fit for work were busy hammering the stones into smaller pieces. When this crude stone bed was ready a giant steam roller appeared from one of the neighboring villages to flatten the surface. Next, some battered old trucks brought black basalt chippings that were spread with shovels on the top and rolled tight. Step by step, in a few Saturdays the whole village was provided with better streets. With "team spirit" a problem was solved in an economical way and without endless parliamentary debates. In the same unbureaucratic fashion and in the interest of all people some other projects were realized, such as the planting of pine trees at a stretch of unused ground along the "Neue Weg" (New Way) at the forest, the laying of the first sewage pipes in certain streets, the public emergency assistance at harvest time after violent storms and rains, and the preparation of an athletics ground together with the "Tommies".

Neighbors' mutual assistance and cooperation was much in demand especially in the community of the refugees from the lost "German Far East". Much was lent and borrowed, starting with a sewing needle with fitting thread up to the hand-operated coffee mill for preparing flour from grain. Actual money was not in demand; even for a time after the currency reform only few people possessed larger amounts, and before it the inflationary Reichsmark was not in demand. “It is not even fit to serve as wallpaper!” people used to remark with grim humor.

The word “hand mill” reminds me of a typical occurrence in this period of starvation. On a warm summer evening, dusk had already set in, the three of us accompanied by our dachshund Zumper took a walk along the apple tree–bordered country road heading east. We were passing the extended rye field of farmer H., which had just been mown the day before. In long rows the sheaves of corn tied with straw ropes were gathered in stacks to soon be taken away and threshed. Suddenly our watchful dog drew our attention to two male human figures who were actually threshing rye. We reassured the startled people. They were also refugees but from the province of East Prussia. The father and son had come by bike from the town to “organize” something. The threshing of corn worked as follows: An old military tarpaulin was stretched over the stubble of the field and one of the bicycles was placed upside down with its rear wheel in the center of it. The job of the son was to hold the front wheel tight between his legs while turning the pedals at the same time. The father held each sheaf sideways at the spokes of the rotating wheel. After stripping them partly from their grain they were returned to the stack. From time to time the corn was shaken together and filled into a sack. I am sure the wife was waiting impatiently at home for the procedure of grinding it to flour after painstakingly removing the husks. Clever people! But we were more honest. My mum was busy as a harvesting help and got the permission for “Stoppeln” (gleaning), which means collecting all the fallen single ears of corn on that stubble field before it was ploughed. The three of us gathered a good quantity within a surprisingly short time. Collecting was rather easy, but the processing later was quite a job. With potatoes it was the same. We always found some forgotten ones after the harvest when digging a bit; it was simply a question of patience.

At harvest time in summer one started to work very early to avoid the heat. Because of the physical drudgery break times were eagerly awaited. Modern harvesting machinery was either none-existent or could not be employed for lack of diesel. Without human workforce the farmer was sold down the river. The farmer's wives prepared a substantial meal and for practical reasons at noon break there was always a varying "Eintopf" (stew) with chunks of pork meat or sliced sausages offered in a huge cauldron. This was kept warm in a "Kochkiste" (a closed wooden chest with handles lined with straw and potato sacks). For breakfast the workforce got slices of rye bread spread with butter or lard and sprinkled with salt. In the afternoon at the "Vesper" break one got bread again with "Mettwurst" (a kind of local Bologna sausage) or homemade plum jam. After some festivities even the remaining cake was used up. In the years of starvation (1946 and 1947) the provision was of course simpler but still better than at home. Beverages were a kind of substitute coffee called "Muckefuck" or fresh pepper- and balm mint tea. Not because of the poor wage that was just pennies (about 0.20 pfennig per hour) but because of the substantial food the field work was much appreciated by the new members of the community. Instead of being paid most refugees asked to be compensated in natural produce.

The excellent tasty full-bodied wholemeal bread was delivered by the village baker. I loved the smell of fresh bread crust in his bakery that had a huge wood-operated oven. Due to the lack of a bakery in some neighboring villages the women still prepared their own bread at home.

In later years after we had moved to the hut we decided to breed rabbits, which multiplied easily. They were really delicious to eat but to "deliver them to heaven" by cutting their throat was always a drama. All rabbits had their proper names and we had great affection for them. I was kept very busy collecting fodder for them as they remained most of the time in their hutch. Outside they soon started by instinct to dig burrows underneath the fences. They loved dandelion, clover and vegetable waste from the garden and were extremely happy to get a carrot from time to time. The slaughtering of the animals was later done by a less-sensitive farmhand living nearby. He had lots of problems with the grammar and orthography of the German language and hated writing. As compensation for his service my mother filled out some forms for him and drew up a couple of official letters.

People can hardly imagine now that in those days small farmers were still using oxen to plough the field or to carry down wagons with tree trunks or firewood from the forest. Working horses like "Hanoverians" were rare, more expensive and sumptuous.

Grandma had induced her neighbors and fellow lodgers always to order their supply of potatoes from my mother's employer farmer, Albert H. After the harvest of potatoes, it was advantageous for him to drive a full wagonload of sacks with his produce, passing the neighboring village and the "Diemardener Warte", a medieval watchtower near the city. As long as it did not collide with my school schedule I was allowed to accompany the farmer. One of the team of horses was rather good-natured and from time to time I was allowed to ride on it, even though there was no saddle available. But the heavy-working horse had such a wide back and a long tasseled mane that it was no problem to stay on it. I always wished at these times that I was small like the "Däumeling" (Tom Thumb) from the fairy tale to hide like him in one of the horse's ears to give him unseen orders where to go. I was told that a queer eccentric fellow, a painter, was residing in the upper room of the abovementioned watchtower. I was always practical-minded so I was scanning the area around the tower for bushes or some kind of primitive toilet shed, but there was none. I racked my brain in order to solve the world-shattering question of the screwball's "big business". Did he sit shamelessly on the parapet of the tower to relieve himself? No, impossible! How could he, a sensitive artist, spoil the side of the tower and its surrounding? Thunderstorms and gales were also a problem. Chamber pot? Balancing it down the steep ladder or stairs everyday… improbable, too troublesome… a bigger container let down with the assistance of a cable drum? Far too much of a bother, and smelly! To climb down only at dark and do it on the open field? That would cause cramps in daytime. As no grown up I asked could solve this enigma I got an unusual idea. The strange hermit on the watchtower must put in long fasting sessions like Mahatma Gandhi, world famous at that time, or like the Indian fakirs. I had taken it into my head to visit the artist one day to solve the mystery of this question, but before I was able to do so, I was told that the artist had left his lofty dwelling and had moved to the city. Probably fed up of not having found a reasonable solution himself he had simply cut and run.

Now I should like to report two examples of the archconservative attitude of the old established villagers: The attractive daughter of a wealthy farmer had, unknown to her parents, an affair with a notorious "petty casanova" during her training time as nurse in a hospital in the city. The result of this "tète-a-tète" was a pretty little boy. First it was kept away with friends far away, because parents and daughter felt extremely embarrassed. The "producer" of the baby had denied any involvement and stayed away. He would not have fit into the picture of a desired son-in-law anyway. The daughter was also moved away for a while until the affair was something of the past and "grass had grown over it", as the Germans use to say. Only then the now grown-up boy was finally accepted at home, but to visitors he was never introduced as the illegal child of the daughter. With the convincing help of an impressive financial dowry and through the assistance of a matchmaker the desired bridegroom was finally found, who generously overlooked the "faux pas" of the famer's appealing young daughter. Thanks to the support of his father-in-law the industrious young husband was able to start a successful automobile trade in the city.

Another "flower of youth" was by the pigheadedness of her well-meaning parents pressing to make – in their eyes – a good match, because the prospective husband owned a successful bakery and confectioner's shop in the city. Her bridegroom was not only much older, but completely different in character. She did not like him. The vivacious and intelligent woman submitted to the union reluctantly but was never happy about her fate. She had another future in mind. Her further misfortune was that her unrestrained and irascible husband suddenly suffered a stroke and was chained to a wheelchair; from now on and for endless years she did her duty and took care of the paralyzed husband and his business. After he had passed away she was lucky to find a congenial second partner. But as happens sometimes in life she sustained again a blow of fate. Her new husband suffered a stroke too and had to be taken care of, moving around in a wheelchair!

One day we got a pleasant surprise. The younger brother of my blood grandfather J. Baron v. R. appeared suddenly unannounced. During our odyssey in and after the war we had lost contact. He drove a battered "Opel" limousine of the early 1930s that still had a starting handle. But anyhow, apart from the permanently disassembled DKW limousine of the pastor, which was jacked up on bricks in the garage, there was not any other car existing in our community. We visibly rose a bit in the esteem of the villagers. It was even more exciting, when it turned out by coincidence, that my granduncle "Jochel" was acquainted with farmer W. from the wartime in Russia. He had been in charge of a special unit in which W. had served too. Together they had fought the Russian partisans, who had continuously and systematically tried to interrupt the long supply routes of the advancing and retreating German army. During the retreat and the dissolution of the unit both men had considered the other one missing or taken POW by the Russians during the chaos before the end of the war. The unexpected reunion was celebrated accordingly. After the irretrievable loss of his landholdings in Silesia, he had taken over from my original grandfather after his death at the end of World War I; he was now without means. His wife Erika was immobilized after a riding accident. There were four children whose given names all started also with "R" like the family name. In addition, there were also a couple of devoted domestic servants and former employees he had to take care of. The helpful commander of his former regiment and a good friend of his, who owned a reactivated textile factory, gave him a job as representative of a larger district. But business was slow, and the people had not enough money to acquire new textiles. In addition, he suffered from a war injury and heart problems. He adored my lively mother. We did everything during his following frequent visits to cheer him up. He instructed me on how to throw knives and rings to hit a target and told me many interesting stories. He was a very educated person. I could ask him anything and he was never at a loss for an answer. One freezing cold morning, after his departure, the old car of Uncle Jochel gave up. It happened on the open road near the village. When even pushing and cranking the starting handle did not help, farmer W. was asked for assistance. With horses harnessed to the Opel, he succeeded to get the vehicle running again. When he visited us again, W. had managed to find a good battery and better sparking-plugs for his car. Unfortunately my granduncle could not enjoy this improvement very long. Shortly after our meeting we got a message that he had suddenly died of a heart attack, but I think grief was the real cause for it.

The countless human fates I was confronted with as a little boy can be estimated while leafing through the visitor's book my mother kept. Unwavering, she also kept writing her diary on cheap brown paper with a lead pencil and later with ink. The entries can only be deciphered with the greatest difficulty because she still used the old-fashioned German scripture/alphabet of that time.

Shortly after our arrival in the pastor's residence in the spring of 1946, the sympathetic and helpful mayor Lipps, according to my mother's request, allotted to us a small piece of land for gardening at the west end of the village near the transformer station. It was there that I got my first instruction in growing vegetables. The first harvest of peas and beans was so abundant that the dried provisions served us well into the next winter. Preserving jars were nonexistent – we got them much later – but we also dried great quantities of apple slices on strings. The creek was not far away, so we had no irrigation problems.

Except in the wintertime, indifferent to storm and rain shepherd K. was guarding his "wool suppliers" somewhere in the area. I met him often when prowling along the "Bramke" creek to watch frogs, grasshoppers, dragonflies and other interesting things. Like so many members of this profession now dying out he was a contemplative, taciturn and nature-loving person. He knew much about the healing properties of plants and about animals, especially birds. He seemed to despise most of his fellow men. Because of his years in the open he could predict the weather quite correctly. When I wanted to know exactly how he did it he said jokingly, "To give a reliable weather forecast is rather simple, you just have to state the opposite propagated by the educated ‘weather frogs’ (meteorologists)!” But later he became serious and explained to me some simple facts about cloud formations, wind direction, changing temperatures and visibility. His black watchdog was restless and was always making his tour around the flock to keep it together.

My brother was very scrawny at the age of twelve years caused by the fatless food of these past years. Through the International Red Cross my mother succeeded in sending him to Auntie “Rieckchen” a lady friend of my grandmother Hitta, who was living in Bern, the capital of Switzerland. During his summer school holidays he was cosseted back to health there. Full of sensational impressions and visibly well fed he came back from his first trip to a foreign and peaceful country with a knapsack and a suitcase full of new children’s wear, chocolate, books and, very strange, a couple of iron studs for climbing boots!!!! An article never seen before which had impressed him. For reasons of shortage of children’s boots the studs could be fitted only years later, but they were proudly shown around in the circle of friends and visitors again and again as a symbol of an intact, orderly world.

Long after the currency reform and the lifting of travel restrictions, and when my brother was already in the boarding school, Auntie R. came to pay us a visit in our primitive hut. One should remember that she had known the still-generous life on the estates of the Silesian nobility, where she had often been the guest of my grandmother and her second husband Count von K. She had first met my mother’s father when he recuperating from a pneumonia which he had caught while a POW in France and from a war wound in a hotel in Davos, Switzerland. The exchange of sick French and German POWs had been made possible by the International Red Cross. She and my grandmother, who came to meet my grandfather, had become very good friends. The friendship was carried over to my generation. I still have contact with her daughter, now an old lady living near Versailles, France.

I am a little bit ahead of my story. We were not living yet in our hut, "Villa Mud", how it was called jokingly later on. There is still something to report of the time, when we enjoyed the hospitality of Uncle Ernst in the parsonage. His adopted son Heinz had shortly before the end of World War II been enlisted for the army but had survived without being taken POW. He suffered from the same handicap as I did: he stammered. His attitude towards his well-meaning parents was so ruffianly that I felt sorry for them. Like many young people at this time he found it difficult to digest the happenings he had experienced in the time of disorder as a very young soldier. Frequently there were heated arguments with his dominating conceited mother Ilse, who did not flinch from slapping his face. In later years, however, he became a reasonable easygoing person. I mentioned already the old defunct DKW automobile parked in the coach house of the parsonage. It had a bodywork made of plywood that was sealed with some kind of black impregnated canvas. The vehicle was the object of Heinz S.'s favorite occupation as he was a born mechanic, skilled in all technical matters. When he was not busy with other assignments he was taking apart and reassembling the car again and again. It seemed to make him happy. The villagers brought him pumps, generators, bicycles, electrical motors, motorcycles and other mechanical appliances for repair. That was the reason that he always had cigarettes, the exchange currency of that time and a criterion for services done. The cigarettes again were exchanged for tools, used spare parts and other sought-after scarce articles. Our mum acquired her first bicycle from Heinz S. that was, however, not paid with cigarettes but exceptionally with cash. I discovered the bill in a pile of old documents. It was a sturdy and heavy bicycle for men – "Diplomat" brand – black in color. It was even equipped with a leather pouch with tools and with an air pump. I was often permitted to accompany my mother, sitting on the luggage carrier in the rear when she rode to the city. We used to carry a rucksack with vegetables for grandma with us, strapped on mum's back or on my front. Saddlebags were not available yet. Of course there used to be a lot of punctures caused mostly by lost horseshoe nails, but Heinz S. had supplied us with sufficient puncture-repair outfits, which we always carried with us. Repairing stuff, outer covers and inner tubes for bicycles were one of the first mass products that were available shortly after the currency reform because of the immense demand. The bicycle was at that time the most popular means of transport in Germany as it still is in China. Before we got ours, we used to walk to Goettingen, taking a shortcut through the mountainous forest above the village. To the center of the city it was about 10 km (6 mi). On our shortcut through the forest we were passing the shooting range and training area of the British forces and the "Ziethen" barracks.

Heinz S. proved himself also as an able organizer, decorator and illumination expert for the community's festive occasions. In later years he made a career as a master mechanic and was working for the General German Automobile Club (ADAC) in Hanover, were his parents had moved after the pastor went into retirement.

My brother's first bicycle was assembled using parts taken from wrecked and abandoned bicycle skeletons. It was artfully decorated with leftover paint. On this exotic means of transport Wolf displayed the most daring acrobatic feats, the easiest being driving straight "freehanded" without holding the handlebars.

Our faithful bodyguard, dachshund Zumper, had taken a fancy to the clergyman and was often sleeping curled up on his lap when he took a rest on his rocking chair after having prepared the Sunday sermon or a burial speech. The animal, however, disliked his wife and wreaked fire and fury when she approached. The dog had sensed that she did not like animals in her living quarters. At one time Zumper incurred also the displeasure of Uncle Ernst.

Unobserved, it jumped on the already-laid dining table and, starved as the dachshund was, devoured the whole rare roast meat already placed there on a serving plate. Just a moment later Ilse and Ernst appeared with the vegetables from the kitchen, but it was too late. The furious woman tried to follow the dog, swinging a carpet beater, but it escaped through the open door with the last slice of roast meat. Later, all including Ilse had something to talk and laugh about. After a long time our Zumper had finally managed to get something substantial to eat.

My godmother, Aunt "Siegrid" from Buedingen, wanted to make me happy and sent me something very useful for my birthday ... a handsaw. I seemed to have nothing better to do and started to try it out at the lower branches of the rare Douglas fir tree at the side of the house's courtyard. The pastor was not very amused about my activities, yet he refrained from giving me a thorough rubdown. After all, the tree was still alive. But he felt it was his duty to enlighten me. He gave me a long lecture about this beautiful tree and others, about their qualities and peculiarities. Since then, he nicknamed me "Sägemueller" (saw miller). With his patient lecturing he probably planted the seed for my pronounced interest in rare trees and botany in general.

I have mentioned already that the forests around were full of military scrap. It originated from the last defensive battles of the German army against the approaching Allied forces. The Americans and the British were especially interested in the secret underground factories for the V2 rockets, which were located not so far away near Bad Lauterberg and the "Mittelwerk Dora" near Nordhausen, both on the slopes of the "Harz" mountain massif. They tried to reach this destination before the "Red Army" could do so, which was still concentrated in taking Berlin. The German soldiers, no longer able or willing to resist this overwhelming pressure had given up their senseless resistance and had simply thrown away or hidden their weapons and equipment and inconspicuously disappeared or surrendered unconditionally. That was a rich source for our collecting activities. There were corroded submachine guns, pistols, rifles, belts of machine-gun ammunition some still in its original steel containers, egg-shaped grenades, hand grenades, rifle ammunition and cartridge cases. Thanks to providence, luck or our careful handling of that hardware nobody was ever harmed in our area. We had been warned by stories from different sources, that children and even adults lost their eyes, limbs and even their lives handling explosives. The son of an acquaintance of my mother lost in this fashion one eye and his left arm. The long, heavy cartridges of the antiaircraft ammunition from the "Erdfalle" were freed from its projectiles that contained the desired lead. The molten lead was used at New Year's Eve to predict the future from the form it created when thrown into a pot with water. The empty projectiles were fixed on the front ends of our javelins. The brass cartridges were filled with bags that contained black tiny explosive chips called cordite, which we used for small secret trial blasts in a stone quarry far away from the village. The quality of the explosive chips and their time of production could be guessed roughly. The "victory" ammunition contained small bags of fine material like silk, the "retreat" ammunition fine paper bags in different shades beige to dark brown. The latter contained explosive chips of a more grayish color, probably an alternative chemical product. The long, empty cartridges still possessed their dangerous percussion caps. The scrap dealer would not accept it in this condition. To defuse them we used an old, disused enamel bucket or something similar, piled a couple of empty cartridges into it and placed them over a fire we had prepared in a stone quarry and took cover. Heated like this the percussion caps ignited one after the other. We had to count carefully not to be hit by a “latecomer”. It made a pretty noise and the side of the bucket was afterward perforated like a sieve. Rifles and pistols held a special fascination for us. The former had often been treated by its last owner in a manner to make them useless by deforming the barrel or its aiming mechanism before throwing it away. Almost everything was corroded, but we tried patiently to make our discoveries work again. The deformed part of the barrel was simply removed with the help of a metal hacksaw Reinhard the farmer’s son had obtained from his father’s workshop. We cleaned the rifle with a wire brush and emery paper and placed it in a length of disused gutter where we treated it with petroleum. The greatest difficulty was to clean the bore of the barrel. The dismantling of the locks of rifles and pistols/handguns was quite easy and we got them working again in most cases after having cleaned, oiled and greased the mechanism. All these activities had to happen in secrecy, unobserved by the grown-ups. When discovered, we risked a thorough caning and loss of our doubtful treasures. Notwithstanding our exertions the success was always uncertain. The bore of the barrels always had traces of corrosion marks difficult to remove with our primitive means. For that very reason we had to be very careful when we undertook our first shooting trials. In the forest we looked for a convenient place with two young trees growing close together. There we fixed the rifle with strings, loaded it and applied the safety catch on disarmed. Next we fastened a string at the lever of the rifle, armed it and took cover behind a tree or a stack of wood and pulled the string. In most trials nothing happened; the ammunition was worthless after having been exposed to humidity for so long. In other cases it really worked, but the barrel or the shortened stump of it exploded.

The damage (shell buster) was caused by corrosion traces inside the barrel. After all our trouble just two working shooting irons remained, one of it with a gunstock and butt I had carved myself as the original was missing. We tried to hit birds and hares with it, but in vain ... that works only with buckshot and a perfect aiming mechanism. Our "arsenal" was carefully camouflaged and wrapped in potato sacks hidden in dry places such as the highest beams of the hayricks and underneath the roofs of the cattle shacks where nobody looked except the pigeons. But piece by piece the whole collection finally found its way to our scrap collector Resebeck, whose descendants are now respected and wealthy recycling industrialists.

In the early years New Year's Eve was celebrated, instead of the usual commercial fireworks, with improvised self-made firecrackers and real explosive grenades, of course, with all due safety precautions by a former infantry man. A farmhand and so-called "Schweizer" who was in charge of the many milk cows of farmer W. knew everything about this subject and did not hesitate to instruct my brother and his friends how to handle and defuse grenades.

We had finally moved into our Villa Mud when a cousin of my mother completely unexpectedly came for a visit. Axel Baron von G. had quite early been released as a POW by the British forces. In Goettingen he had just matriculated at the university for studies in ethnology and German philology. It was a great joy for my mother. They had spent their youth together at my grandfather's place. In the following years he often came to visit us by bike on weekends and we were always looking forward to hear his interesting news. Before the war started he had been called back for his military service from East Africa, where he had been working on a farm. During his time in present Tanzania he had been busy studying the history, customs, culture and present living conditions of the native tribes and could tell amazing stories about it. On one of his visits he surprised us boys while we were handling some of our rusty weapons and also discovered some ammunition hidden underneath the hut and in our treehouse. He took the whole dangerous lot and threw it into the bordering fire-brigade pond. As compensation for the loss he told us about his personal experiences during the wartime as artillery officer in the desert, in Russia and finally in Italy. He instructed us about how the natives in Africa prepared bows and arrows and showed us how to use them properly. Together we fixed up a primitive crossbow and were quite successful in hitting our self-made straw practice target. Uncle Axel was always starved, living in the city and was happy to get some reasonable "chow" prepared by my mother. His student provisions seemed to have been very mean and his financial situation limited. His small attic room in the city had just a small barrel-shaped furnace to cook on and to heat the place in the cold season. I used to accompany him into the forest to gather a sack full of firewood and also to look for some mushrooms, which he took home.

My brother wanted to be a forester when he grew up. He was chasing hares even those with skirts. My dream, however, was to be the driver of a steam locomotive, but our ideas concerning professions were always changing later on as happens to most children. There exists a picture of mine taken at a "Kirmes" procession (harvest festival) where I am disguised as "Hans im Glück" (lucky dog), globetrotter, a really exciting occupation.

Sometime or other there developed a plague of sparrows all over the country. To fight it our community paid five pennies for every killed bird of this kind. For this reason slings became very popular. Our type was cut from a forked branch carved around where the rubber elastic band (we used the sealing rings of preserving jars) was fixed at both "V" branches with copper wire. The bands again were fixed to a leather patch to hold the shooting pebble. For a better hold the grip was wrapped with a piece of a bicycle tire inner tube or wrapped up with a string. It took a lot of training to hit a sitting sparrow with a pebble stone, but we managed to collect a decent number of prey. Consequently the turnover of sweets rose in our village store. These were displayed on the counter in a huge glass jar with a sideways opening and were taken out with a wooden trowel. No child could resist the temptation, but we brothers always kept some coins for our saving boxes.

Plastic bags were nonexistent. People went shopping equipped with a basket or a fabric shopping bag, string net or the long-valued knapsack. The purchased goods such as groats, flour, sugar and salt were wrapped in pages of newspapers or were filled into conical or, later, square brown paper bags. When my mother went shopping I usually accompanied her to help carry the purchases. The shop owner Mrs. Lindau always slipped some sweets into my hands. Later, "lollies" in bright color (long sugar bars with a wooden handle) became popular. Sacrificing my minimal savings I got in this store my first Christmas gift for mum: a lemon and a cognac glass. The lemon was the first one I had ever seen. It was smelling so exotic and looked so beautiful, but to be honest I had not the slightest idea of its use. The cocktail glass, however, had a practical purpose. A visitor had given my mother a bottle with an impressive label and on special occasions she served herself only sparingly, sipping the liquid from one of our ugly scratched tin cups.

Besides collecting pennies for decimating sparrows we could earn some more coins on the fields in the springtime at the job of weeding young seedlings of sugar beet and fodder turnips. The single plants growing in rows needed space, so the weak and surplus ones were pulled out to guarantee a good crop later on. This work was not a hard one, but you had to be very attentive, precise and careful not to step on the plants behind you and destroy them. I remember that one year all school children together with the schoolmaster were employed for this job.

When my mother went to Goettingen to arrange something and also spent some time waiting at the dentist, I spent my time sitting at the fountain in front of the city hall, where the pretty bronze monument of the "Gänseliesel" (geese-herding maiden) was displayed or on the stairs in front of the dentist's practice in the busy "Theaterstrasse" (Theatre Street). In the springtime I was equipped with a basket selling small bunches of wild flowers such as violets, marguerites, harebells or lilies of the valley, which I had collected myself, and I charged ten pennies per bunch. Before Christmas I sold self-made straw stars, gold-painted nuts and silver-painted pine cones with copper wire loops as decorations for the Christmas tree.

Very exciting for us children was a puppet show, the first one any of us had ever seen. The entertainer had rented the big hall of the other "Gaststätte" (public house) for the performance, which was fully booked even with grown-ups. It was so funny that I secretly slipped my savings into my pocket, walked all alone to the city and acquired a cheap foldable puppet-theater stand in the toy section of the newly opened department store Karstadt. It consisted of pressed cardboard covered with multicolored and funny decorated paper and the "stage" opening had a green curtain. There was just enough money left to buy a crocodile, the most exotic figure. At home again I was of course admonished by mum, but later she and grandma Hitta made dresses for the figure heads of Punch, the king, the princess, the devil and so on which I had started to carve from soft poplar wood. The material I got from our helpful cabinet maker S. The heads were also painted in lively colors. I developed a considerable proficiency in entertaining the youngsters of my own age. They were an easygoing appreciative audience at those free shows at home. My wooden green crocodile with white teeth was the star. "Caspar" (Punch) had even the job of polishing its rows of teeth with my own toothbrush. Brushing our teeth at this time was still a problem; tooth paste was not yet available in our shop. We improvised using salt or pounded chalk organized from the school. Schoolmaster B. must have wondered about the high expenditure of writing chalk.

There was a period when we were infected by the "Red Indian" virus. The old, hollow lime tree above the limestone quarry at the eastern end of the village, where the store of the voluntary fire brigade was situated and where the "Neue Weg" (New Way) started was the gathering place of our gang. On some occasions there happened to be rows with the "band of robbers" from the other side of the village. Using bird and poultry feathers we had put together impressive headdresses. Bow and arrow and a wooden battle axe formed our equipment. To paint our faces we used chalk from school and soot from the oven or from a cork bottle stopper held over a candle light. Already after our first year in school when we had learned to read and write, we developed a simple cipher to exchange "world shaking" messages with each other. It was done like this: The letter "A", for example, became an "X" and "B" a "Q" and so on. The numbers were mixed up in the same manner. In the case, our opponents had watched us hiding messages underneath a certain stone or in a tree's knot hole; they were unable to decipher it. Everywhere we had built our secret hiding places. There were several simple tree houses made of boards and branches of trees. Deep in an undergrowth we had built a more sophisticated hiding place on ground level. It was surrounded by a kind of palisade. Inside was a conical hut made of straight branches, open on the top to release the smoke of the small fireplace. The construction looked like an Indian wigwam.

The underground place was a rectangular pit we had dug

near the New Way within the forest. We had covered it with logs from a pile of beech tree firewood nearby and disguised it with layers of sods, branches and leaves. It even had a trap door. But it was wasted time and energy. Down inside it was humid and smelly, and everything corroded or attracted mildew. We soon gave it up.

While the girls stayed at home taking care of their dolls, sewing dresses for them, helping in the kitchen preparing cake, playing "Himmel und Erde" (heaven and earth) outside, training with the skipping rope, braiding each other's hair and drawing pictures, the boys had other pastimes. As long as there was no thunderstorm, hail or lasting rain, we were roaming around outside. We played, for example, fire brigade. We dammed up the creek running through the valley down from the village. Somewhere we had organized a hand operated air-raid pump with a long hose. We all carried military steel helmets we had found in the forest with red lead paint used to protect iron farm equipment against corrosion. We behaved very professionally when we extinguished the burning pile of wood we had gathered. The commander of our brigade was Reinhard H. He was very satisfied when we shouted "Yes Sir! Right away captain!" when he gave his orders.

In an easterly direction at the foot of the "Hengstberg" (stallion mountain) and at the side of a pasture hidden behind bushes existed an extended natural pond. In the nearby forest we had discovered two empty fuel reserve tanks dropped by allied bomber planes. These aluminum containers resembled giant bombs but were very light. We dragged them to the pond. With appropriate tools from Rainer's father's workshop we made square openings on the tops and placed seating boards inside. Next we joined the two tanks with bolts exactly where they had been connected to the wings of the aircraft. After we had made two rowing oars we could start to play pirates. When we found that the strange boat did not move fast enough, we equipped it with a mast, an old, tarred tarpaulin as a sail and a rudder behind.

“Krieters Kopp” was a further location of interest. In the wintertime it was a favorite place for toboggan runs. In the very first winter in the village my brother took me there with a borrowed sledge. Together with many others we enjoyed very much racing down the slope, I sitting in the front. On one of the trips he went down in the wrong direction and could not avoid hitting a barbed wire fence. He was unscathed but I suffered a torn open lip and chest. The lip had to be stitched by a surgeon. Even today I have a barely visible mark across my chest, a souvenir of that winter. In the summertime the top of its hill with a couple of oak trees was the breeding place of the extremely rare stag beetles with their impressive catchers fighting against each other. They returned every year to the same place.

In the springtime there was often an invasion of cockchafer beetles. Nowadays this species of beetles has nearly died out because of the intensive use of chemical products for agriculture. The cockchafers seemed to be a delicacy for the chicken. They were gathered in buckets and fed to the poultry. The eggs the chicken laid afterward had a different taste from the regular ones, but of course not bad. The farmers did not like them because they caused some damage, but the main staple of those beetles were the young leaves of the beech trees. The most beautiful examples of this species had special marks at their front and had a certain collector’s value for us boys. One was very rare and was named “king”; it could be exchanged against several “millers” and even more “beggar men”. We kept these scrambling animals in cigar boxes, which we had provided with air holes and filled with fresh beech leaves. We used the inner drawers of the matchboxes “Welthölzer Blau” to construct mini-wagons, harnessed the cockchafers in front with looped threads and trained them to move straight on a white chalked line. We let them starve before racing competitions and tempted them with fresh beech tree leaves to come forward. It was real fun, when the betting started and the participants behaved as if being at a horse race.

Always before 10:00 a.m. on Sunday mornings an invasion of villagers came from all directions aimed at the protestant church. "With bag and baggage" dressed in dark colors and the kids exceptionally scrubbed clean by means of curd soap, everybody who could move, equipped with hymnbook and small change took their places on the benches to listen devoutly to the eloquent sermon of the pastor. Those lectures often took direct reference to actual occurrences in the community and caused some members of the audience to blush and hide their face behind the hymnbook. Schoolmaster B. played the organ or directed the church choir. Then the collection bag was passed around. I often assisted the pastor after the church was over to sort out and count the contents of the velvet collection bag and the collecting box at the church's exit. Frequently I found aluminum coins of no value from the recent "millennium", buttons and corroded washers ... hard currency was still scarce! The children's service was never boring. Pastor S., who had been a missionary in East Africa in the past, to drum the Lutheran principles into the heads of his native flock, had a masterly way of attracting our attention. When he lectured nobody fell asleep. Noah and his Ark, Sodom and Gomorrah, David and Goliath, Cain and Abel were all eminent personalities and places, and Abraham and Moses were superstars. His wife Ilse, who often took his place when he was too busy to teach us children, turned more to the parables and the Passion and the suffering of our Lord. In her lectures about the beloved Jesus Christ the color "pink" was dominant. Very popular and objects of exchange were little pictures with short explanations portraying happenings from the Bible, which were always distributed after the children's sermons.

I contrived several times to climb stealthily on to the top of the church tower that was out of bounds for all. I was fascinated by the bells, the ear-splitting sound they made when they were struck at each hour, and the rattling of the enormous old-fashioned clockwork and the beautiful view from above through the ventilation apertures of the spire. The bells were still operated from downstairs by means of a long rope. The belfry was the home of numerous swallows other birds. Bats were hanging from the crossbeams. They seemed to have gotten used to the sound of the bells. Once I scared an owl that hissed at me indignantly because of this breach of peace. It smelled beastly, and scattered everywhere were the remains of its victims and the drippings of all occupants.

Once it happened that I was locked in the church and I felt like a prisoner, but after the first panic I discovered a way to escape through a high window. The old-fashioned oversized key for the main entrance of the church was so impressive that I imagined St. Peter to have a similar one suspended from the rope of his cowl for the gate of heaven. St. Peter was a rather popular figure for us children, being in charge of rain and sunshine. When there happened to be a downpour we used to remark irreverently, "Saint Peter is piddling again!" Donar and Wotan, the Teutonic gods of the past, whom we had heard about already, were in charge of the more violent natural phenomenon.

A real sensation had been the installation of the new bells with all its technical expenditure. The former bells had probably been taken away during the wartime and molten down as material for the "final victory".

Weddings were a matter where the whole population was involved. Large trays with already-prepared dough for the cakes were carried to the baker K. to be placed into the oven. Sometimes I helped with carrying them and as reward I got a slice of bread with plum jam or dripping. The womenfolk were busy with cooking and decorating. From the big chest was taken the wedding dress handed down from the mother or grandmother and smelling of moth balls, and it was altered if necessary. The same happened with the frock coat of the men. The bridegroom was still wearing a black top hat like a chimney sweep. The dark dresses were aired and cleaned with substitute coffee. The cleaning was still done with traditional simple methods.

When the couple left the church, little girls nicely dressed all in white were carrying the train of the wedding dress and others were scattering flowers from wicker baskets in front of the procession. The whole way up to the bride's home was covered with scattered twigs of fir trees. Marriages were preferably done in the finer times of the year except in cases were the bride was already in the family way and it was urgent to marry her off to avoid a birth out of wedlock, a great embarrassment in those years.

It was a striking fact that most of the birthdays were celebrated in the last four months of the year. It had a simple reason. In the winter season, with shorter days and less to do outside the villagers went to bed much earlier. There was then no entertainment such as we have nowadays. People read a lot, but in the first postwar years power cuts were frequent and not every household had electricity.

In the springtime the little girls loved to prepare garlands of wild flowers and wear them on their heads. At confirmations, weddings and on Martinmas we children moved in groups to the appropriate house or through the whole village from door to door and sang a song and recited a short, popular poem. It was the custom to supply us with sweets or cake, which were prepared for such occasions. At the lantern festival we processed singing through the darkness with hollowed-out pumpkins in which we had cut openings for eyes, nose mouth and ears. Candles illuminated the inside of the yellow shining pumpkins that were carried on long sticks. Later, foldable paper lanterns in different colors and shapes were introduced. This children's festival had nothing to do with the Anglo American Halloween.

The most exciting outdoor festival, however, was the annual parish fair called "Kirmes" (church fair). For this occasion a large procession was organized. The horse boxes and wagons were decorated with spruce and fir green garlands interwoven with flowers and were dedicated to different topics of daily life or fairy tales. Even the draught horses had bunches of flowers fixed to the leather harness behind their ears. All those actively participating were disguised. My classmate and girlfriend went as a shepherdess, and for lack of a tame sheep she was accompanied by the goat of her grandmother. I went as "Lucky dog" and was photographed together with a painter and a chimney sweep. This "Kirmes" attracted a few show- and tradesmen with their shooting galleries, merry-go-rounds, sweet stalls and so on. My favorite was the boat swing. It was a special task to swing the small boat completely around standing the fraction of a second upside down on the top while turning a complete circle. Due to the centrifugal power one could not fall down, but often the stomach, not used to such a treatment, revolted. The prizes won when throwing balls successfully on pyramids of empty tin cans or when shooting on small white clay pipes with an air rifle were without exception "Kitsch" (rubbish). The gingerbread in form of a heart with icing decoration and remarks like "I love you forever!" and "My little sweetheart!" and so on are still "en vogue".

The primitive wooden outside toilet "Herzhäuschen" or ordinarily called "Donnerbalken" (thunder beam) erected at a distance from our hut was a comfortable place, except in deep winter. The seat was made of carefully planed pinewood, and the opening even had a round cover with handle. It also offered "air conditioning" because the side panels consisted of crude firwood boards, which still possessed their bark on the outside. During our sessions we could observe the surrounding through the gaps between the boards. During periods of temperatures below 0°C (freezing) there was always an axe and a spade available leaning beside the seat, to sever the frozen "Mount Everest", growing more and more toward the opening. There were still no toilet paper rolls available in our village store in the years we were living in Villa Mud, so we used as in the parsonage carefully cut square pieces of newspaper from old editions of the *Goettinger Tageblatt* (*Daily Mail*) placed in a basket. Many guests used to stay endlessly in our "chambre separée" to study the countless anecdotes, jokes, wise sayings, caricatures and spectacular reports we had diligently cut out from newspapers, illustrated papers and other publications and fixed with drawing-pins to the boards. The ambience was further improved by the ripple of the creek that was passing just behind, the lowing and ruminating sound of the cows, the neighing of the horses and the concert of the birds. In those years the latter were more numerous and existed in a much greater variety of species. The reasons were the more natural living conditions and a healthier environment. Countless swallows had their nests in every cowshed, the sky lark was floating in the wind over the cornfields and the steel-blue kingfisher was around. Chemical products for the use in the agriculture were for years not available, and there was no hard cash. The production of mass chemicals had not started yet. The Allies had ordered the dissolution of former combines. The factories, especially in the Soviet-occupied zone in the East, had been dismantled and shipped to Russia and raw materials were not delivered for financial reasons ... sorry, I am a little bit off the track. Let us return to our "observation point", where later the "last before last" edition of the local *Daily Mail* could often be studied, which the pastor let us have after having read it. When a guest came he was tactfully informed about the peculiarities of our "chambre separée" in which robins used to build their nests right underneath the roof. The most important was that the door was closed correctly by means of a hook and to shout "Already occupied!" in case somebody approached it. If we wanted to tease somebody, we locked the door from outside and opened only when the "insider" ceased grumbling and started to beg and probably promised us some sweets.

Near the toilet beside the fence we had dug a small pit for the nearly nonexistent refuse, covered with some branches. There we buried a couple of tiny young ducklings, which our dachshund Jockel had unobserved killed and started to carry home. When the loss was discovered by the hot-tempered owner some hours later, our dachshund was suspected right away. He came and looked for feathers everywhere and after having inspected the body of our dog for traces of a "duckling meal" in vain, he left frustrated without proof. We did not compensate him for the damage, as we had our good reasons.

When the denazification campaign of the Allies came to an end and printing paper was again available, the local newspaper appeared again, in a limited number, on cheap yellowish paper. It went of course from hand to hand which were, after reading it, black from the simple printing ink. It would be rather amusing to study the first postwar editions to get a picture of the general situation. At the start the press was still censored as before. Free information and the expression of opinion was not right away permitted even in the zones occupied by the western democracies. There were some embarrassing facts concerning them they did not want to be spread. That only changed when the "Luftbrücke" (airlift) to the encircled Berlin was started due to differences with the Soviets and when the Federal Republic of Germany was founded. The greatest interest was attracted not by the international news and other headlines but by the small printed advertisements on the last pages that touched upon elementary life, like "Exchange mattress for man's winter coat/slim figure 185 cm" or "Books for provisions" and "Who can supply news about my missing husband?" (detailed information followed). People spared no pains of making long trips with a pram or a handcart to get bigger items of desire. As the telephone was still pure luxury and in many cases did not work, many of the interested parties arrived too late at the disposer's place and had to leave again disappointed and empty-handed. Much attention was also given to the job column and the culture news. Cultural events distracted people from the daily drudgery. When the "Deutsches Theater", the local playhouse in Goettingen, opened its gates again and cheap subscriber tickets were available, the house was always fully booked. The university city was fortunate to get the famous Heinz Hilpert from Berlin as theater manager, who also appeared on the stage as actor in leading parts. For villagers, however, it was quite a task to go to a concert, a play, a lecture or a recitation. When alone, one took the bicycle. A real problem was theft. For this very reason a new kind of business developed: bicycle-storage halls, but those closed in the evening long before the performances were finished.

People who wanted to travel and those who wanted to join a cultural happening had to walk along the Brahmke creek to the station Steinsmuehle of the "Gartetalbahn" (Garte-Valley-Train) 3 km away, a narrow-gauge line with a train that did not offer a frequent service. The steam locomotive of the small train announced its arrival by an uninterrupted tolling of its bell and occasional signals with its whistle before it crossed a street. One time we witnessed that the train was forced to stop because some cows had to be removed from the tracks with the assistance of the passengers. They had found a place in the fence, where the barbed wire had been damaged and they had used the opening to make an excursion into the close surrounding. The train ride to Goettingen took about an hour, because the train had to stop at a couple of other points and was quite slow. The fare was collected on the train. At harvest time the locomotive was even slower because it had to pull some additional freight wagons loaded with sugar beet, potatoes and grain. The compartments with wooden benches were sooty and full of fumes not just because of engine but because of the countless male pipe smokers, who enjoyed their homemade "Knaster" (shag/stinking weed). The small train arrived at a sidetrack at the city's railway station. There we had to cross the huge place in front of it, then pass "Gebhard's Hotel", the most renowned lodging of the university city, then walk to the center crossing the Leine Kanal (canal) and further on to the roundabout in front of the theater. Opposite the impressive building of the Deutsches Theater was the ethnological institute with its small but marvelous museum. The cheapest places in the theater were in the upper tier, from where one could not see the stage so well. The even cheaper and most disadvantageous area was the "Bumms" and offered just a few standing places for viewing reasons. It was often crowded by us and some parsimonious students. At the end of the play we had to return home walking; there were no more trains. It was pleasant to walk in the summer nights through the forest underneath a clear-star-and-moonlit sky talking about the play we had just seen and other matters. Sometimes we met wild boars, deer and foxes on their search for food and prey. When alone, we stayed with our grandma and took the morning train back home.

Cinemas were soon opened again. After the currency reform we got pamphlets at the cashier's place for 10 pence each in which the story of the movie just presented was explained in detail. The youngsters collected those leaflets and exchanged them with each other.

When we had bad weather we stayed in the barn of farmer H., chasing mice in the grain store, or we talked to the animals in the warm cowshed or horse stable and helped to clear out the manure and feed the hungry creatures. All the horses and cows had their own names in the pigsty however just the sow and the boar. There were too many sucklings. But then a fast-spreading animal disease (foot and mouth disease) reduced their numbers drastically and caused a lot of headaches to the farmers. The farmer's wife taught me to milk the cows and I was also allowed to help make butter with the churn. One cannot imagine how good homemade butter tastes. Even the farmers don't know it anymore; they buy their butter in the supermarkets like everybody else. Another delicacy was the thick skin that floated on fresh cooked milk. We children loved to romp around in the hayloft. Underneath the hidden beams the stored hay was not so tightly packed; there we established a labyrinth of passages where we moved along like moles and played hide-and-seek. Afterward we were full of dust; our noses and ears were blocked, and grass seeds and hay stalks were in the hair, the shirts and trousers. It was itching and pricking a lot. Sometimes we discovered chicken eggs in the hay and in the straw of the barn and soon we knew the preferred places where the free-roaming chicken laid its eggs. The "undisciplined" poultry could not get used to lay their eggs properly in the boxes in the chicken pen, and the farmer's wife always had problems collecting them. We helped her search for the eggs. As a reward for our findings we got some homemade sweets from the big tin box that was normally locked away in the cupboard.

"La haute cuisine" in times of distress

Usually cooking recipes start with the words "You take ...!" But what to do when about nothing is available or cannot be paid for? One is forced to look for alternatives. Already in wartime when provisions and other things were rationed and long queues were lined up in front of shops, the people racked their brains to find something to supplement their miserable diet. There were of course ration cards to control the supply of victuals, but rarely was everything listed available ... "paper is patient!" Especially in the cities the greatest problem was to get meat and all kinds of fat. That was mostly going in tinned form to the different frontlines to supply the fighting armies. Much was "gehamstert" (German for marmot) hoarded, that means people traveled long distances by bike or train to the countryside and tried to get something in exchange for other goods of mostly daily use. This situation helped also to create "black markets" in spite of the threatened penalties. In the countryside illegal "black" slaughtering was common. The policemen and other representatives of the authorities often closed their eyes confronted with this situation; their families were starving too. The exchange trade ended soon after the new hard currency of the Deutsche Mark was introduced in June 1948.

In the years after the end of the war and well into the 1950s our provisions were modest but, compared with now, extremely healthy. No supermarket or five-star "de luxe" hotel can offer those strange things that our mother was able to prepare by magic and place on the table after our collecting tours. I have not forgotten this time and still enjoy especially in spring and early summer the daily varying delicious combinations of wild herbs and greens like dandelion, cuckoo flower, ground ivy, peppermint, balm mint, goatsfoot, wild mustard, forest garlic, winter cress, comfrey, daisy, watercress, shepherd's purse, wild hops, coltsfoot, burdock root, sorrel, wood sorrel, chickweed and some more whose names I don't have in English. Of some of the plants the roots are also edible; they were chopped together with sprouts and leaves and rolled into fine pancakes and fried. They looked like Chinese Spring Rolls but were much better. Our salads were also of continuously changing combinations. Chopped finely, the different herbs and leaves could be mixed with potato salad, yellow turnips and cheese curd or mixed with chive from the garden spread on our breakfast slices of bread. For winter we stored some long-lasting cabbage, and when we later got a stoneware pot, we got our own "Sauerkraut".

There is one field plant that even grows underneath the snow and is frost-resistant, that is rape. The leaves are very tasty and can be cooked like spinach or eaten as salad. With its yellow flowers the fields look beautiful in summer. The seeds contain a good cooking oil nowadays also used as "bio"-diesel-oil.

Our universal stew had a varying composition and consistence, but it always kept its green color. Flour was something difficult to get in the first years, so it was stretched with flour grated from the dried roots of thistles or potato starch. Even later we were probably the most frequent customers at the village baker asking for leftover dried bread and hard rolls. Mixed with our "magic flour" and boiled potatoes we used them soaked in water to prepare dumplings or soufflé or grated to sprinkle fried dishes. Capers were made from buds of marsh marigold, dandelion, nasturtium and daisy and preserved in homemade apple vinegar. The dried roots of the wild chicory with its blue blossoms were chopped and roasted together with barley grains in an old iron pan or pot and milled or ground to powder. That was our famous "Ersatzkaffee" (substitute coffee). I should also mention we collected mushroom in certain areas. Some we found nearly every year; others only occasionally. Those we could not eat right away were dried on strings and kept for winter. There was one kind that was called "Steinpilz"; in English it is simply called "edible mushroom". It was my favorite one fried together with onions, a very rare delicacy nowadays.

Thistles are considered a bothersome weed. When very young and soft their stings have to be eliminated with the help of scissors, then the leaves are chopped and fried together with onions, a tasty decoration on fried eggs and on mashed potatoes. The base of the thistle flower when cooked tastes like artichokes.

My favorite menu that time was spinach of young stinging nettles and wild garlic, mashed potatoes, fried eggs all sprinkled with fried thistle and onions and some spoons of preserved apple puree. If I had the choice and was offered this simple menu nowadays, no “Chateaubriand” could tempt me. Then there were the young filled and rolled coltsfoot leaves bound together with sewing thread and fried in the pan.

I have already mentioned that cooking and salad oils were almost unavailable in the first couple of years; the farmers had their lard and some homemade butter for their own use. Right in the first autumn in the village we went into the beech forests in search of the tiny triangle seeds of this tree. These beech nuts are extremely difficult to collect because of their small size and their brown camouflage color. They contain a very good oil, today unknown.

It took some days until we had assembled a reasonable quantity. We gave them to a villager, who had a special hand-operated press to extract the precious oil. As compensation for his service he kept the residues to feed his chickens and ducklings, and we also shared some oil with him.

Dessert was determined by the time of the year. When no rhubarb, berries or fruit were available we still had dried or preserved fruit. Something special was the marmalade of stewed hips from the hawthorn bush, but the preparation of this tiny red fruit was difficult. First, the dried remains of the former blossoms and the stem had to be removed. Next, it had to be slit open and the hairy seed had to be taken out with a small spoon or knife. The seeds were dried together with some of the opened hips and used for tea that had a nice red color. Cake was not often on our table; it was reserved for special occasions if ever the ingredients were available. Occasionally guests brought something that was missing in the “kitchen”. To prepare berry blancmange our mother got “island moss” from the forest. It must be the ugly silver-grayish-looking dried-out plants, which don’t contain any more bitter agents. They are ground to powder and possess absorption qualities necessary for making jelly together with sugar.

In late spring we prepared the traditional "Maibowle" (a cold alcoholic drink) prepared with fresh woodruff that grew in the beech forests, sugar and white wine. At an earlier time, when white wine was not available, we prepared our own one using the yellow flowers of dandelion, yeast from the baker and sugar. It took a couple of weeks of fermentation until the wine was drinkable and contained some alcohol. When the sugar supply was normal again and we could even get a glass balloon with a plug and siphon we could prepare some really good-tasting fruit wines. The best was from wild yellow plums (mirabelle) and sloe the fruit of the black thorn bush that had also a wonderful violet color.

Mum prepared also a lot of marmalade, jellies, jams and fruit juices. That had become possible because our resourceful auntie "Fiete", who studied law in Goettingen, had organized a battered aluminum contrivance to prepare juice by means of steam and another one to preserve glass jars with vegetable and fruit. Our starved guests from the city got always some samples of our products when they left, but they knew that they had to provide us with some empty jars with fitting rubber sealing rings, something a bit difficult to get at those days. When we were lucky to have enough flour at our disposition we prepared our own bread just for fun. We mixed the dough with the kernels of nuts. The loaves were round as we used tin cans as baking forms. The sides had to be flat and had to be brushed inside with fat to get the bread out easily when it was ready. The slices of the brown bread rolls were roasted on the hot top of the cast iron oven hob. It smelled and tasted wonderful.

When I skim through the countless actual publications and read pseudoscientific articles about slimming-down programs and about health food I can just shake my head and smile. Unaware and forced by poverty and bad times we were living extremely healthily ... no Hindu or Buddhist monk could have done better.

There was no water supply for our “Villa Matsch”. About 300 m uphill existed a covered well equipped with an old-fashioned iron pump. The water for cooking and for laundry had to be carried in buckets all the way down. To go there I first had to slip through the barbed wire fence, balance over the board crossing the creek and walk up the pasture passing cows or horses to climb through two fences with barbed wire again. One can imagine that the return trip with full buckets was quite a task. Water used for other means was taken from the dammed-up creek. Larger quantities of hot water for our compulsory Saturday evening bath was prepared over an open fire outside our hut in a large zinc cauldron with two handles. Our tiny “Hexe”-stove was too small for such a job except in winter when the oven was in action the whole day. When the weather was good we took a bath outside standing in the tub and showering each other with a watering can.

In times of bad weather our universal tub was placed besides the entry door of our “palace”. There was also a round wooden block to split firewood with the ax, and to sit on, and a towel was hanging on a nail. Before entering the “saloon” we were obliged to clean our mud-covered feet.

When the rain drummed onto the tarred paper of the roof and beat noisily against the panes or the shutters of both windows and we had distributed some pots underneath the few leaks, we could turn to our homework or our “Bastelei” (handicraft as hobby). In the first class we practiced writing still on an “environment-friendly” slate with a wooden frame and a slate pen. The only disadvantage was that such a thing broke easily when dropped.

In my free time I used to carve a lot with a fitting knife Uncle Axel had given me. Using the thick bark of an old yellow pine tree I carved little boats that even had masts and paper sails. We tried them out in the pond in front or in our creek. In the springtime when the thin bark of the ash tree was still soft and easy to take away, I carved elaborately decorated spears, bows and a walking stick for an old uncle of ours. Aunt Eva taught us the art of paper folding and drawing. Her efforts were not in vain. We also composed a lot of nonsense; the important thing was that it was a rhyme. We liked to play theater when an exacting audience was present. Then we imitated the stammering son of the pastor, really no problem for me as I was a natural talent that stuttered too. The next targets were the herald of the village, Schoolmaster B. giving lessons in local history, Pastor S.'s admonition on his pulpit on Sundays, the drunken and babbling farmhand R. and our country doctor from the next village. Objects for our acting existed "en masse". When alone we annoyed our dachshund by imitating animal voices or barking like dogs of different breeds. Casual passing villagers must have thought our hut to be an animal asylum or a loony bin, but we were well known for our foolish actions.

Together with our mum we played "Halma" and "Mühle", two German board games that we had made ourselves, including the figures and stones. Soon a card game "Schwarzer Peter" was added, a present of my aunt Siegrid. Much later, Uncle Axel taught me to play chess, which was extremely fascinating.

Friedhelm B., an older boy, was in charge of the more sophisticated handiworks. He showed us how to construct model gliders and a primitive radio receiver, but that needs to be explained in more detail: In a cigar box or something similar one fixed a glass tube. On one side there was a quartz crystal and on the other side a brush-like metal feeler both with insulated copper wires. Those were connected with the two poles of a square torch battery and again with a primitive cheap headset. The search for a radio station by means of moving the feeler over the crystal could start. The reception was weak when we were lucky enough to find a station. FM did not exist yet. The parts for this "poor people's radio" were very cheap. It was very popular. Next we constructed a working battery-operated electrical doorbell. Less demanding was our telephone. A fine hole was made at the center of the bottom of two empty tin cans. A length of copper wire we had rescued from an electrical coil belonging to a crashed fighter aircraft was inserted from outside the cans through the holes and fixed around a nail, so that it could not slip back; next the two participants pulled at both sides until the wire was taut and did not touch anything. Now you could speak and listen into the cans. The sound was transferred by oscillations caused by the voice. It was just a physical gimmick of no practical use. We could have comfortably shouted to each other.

At the "DM" time another uncle sent me for my birthday a used metal construction kit with aluminum moldings, angle plates, rubber wheels, brass screws and nuts, a screwdriver and a tiny spanner. There was no limit to my creativity. My most sophisticated construction was a carriage with four wheels. On its top I fixed an empty cartridge and a load of lead. It was filled with a mixture of sugar and cordite (gunpowder). On a level stretch of the newly tarred country road outside the village I ignited the charge of my rocket car and enjoyed it when it raced along the road leaving a fire tail behind. When I knew it was working I repeated the experiment proudly in front of my playmates.

An exciting matter was the erection of the maypole. Beforehand a wreath of fir green decorated with colored ribbons and a couple of prizes like a bottle of brandy, sausages, pralines and so on were fixed on its top. The most skilled boys and young men tried to climb the smooth-planed pole to get one of the prizes, stimulated by the shouting and hand-clapping of especially the female spectators. The first who managed the difficult task had the largest choice. It was not an easy job and most of the climbers gave up halfway. The children competed with each other at "Sackhuepfen" (sack race), "Blinde-Kuh" (blindman's buff), "Eierlaufen" (egg-and-spoon race) or horseshoe throwing.

For the thirsty villagers, fresh draught beer from oak barrels or brown bottles with white patent stoppers and cold “Bowle” with woodruff or “Schnaps” (spirit) were offered. The children got raspberry lemonade and apple juice, or they dissolved tablets of different varieties of tastes like orange, lemon, peach, woodruff and so on in a glass of cold water to get a fizzy drink. Coca-Cola and other soft-drink brands had not yet started their advertisement campaigns and were not popular.

Contrary to our times with government health warnings on tobacco products, men smoked a lot, and pipe smoking was the most economical way. At the end of the war and the first ensuing years the stubs of the filterless cigarettes and cigar ends were collected inconspicuously, chopped fine and mixed with fermented leaves of the chestnut tree or those from blackberries. Anyway, everybody had his personal recipe for the best mixture. Later people got seeds from the nearby tobacco-growing region “Eichsfeld” and started to grow their own “Knaster” (stinking weed) in their gardens. The long, fully developed leaves were fermented and hung in bundles on the southern walls of shacks, barns and the framework houses for drying. With a hand-operated device that looked like a mincer and was fixed to a workbench the tobacco was cut into fine strips and was ready for use. We children wanted to imitate the adults and smoked the porous stems of a liana-like climbing plant, “Backisbart”, that at certain places grew over bushes and trees. The effect of smoking those fags was that we were feeling unwell or we got diarrhea or both, which we endured with poise, because now we were “real men”. Later we made ourselves pipes from hollowed-out chestnuts or dried corn cobs and stems of the elder bush that had a very soft white marrow easy to take out by means of a hooked wire or the spoke of a bicycle wheel and secretly smoked “organized” real tobacco.

One day in spring my brother and I, while roaming around, found a baby rook (Saatkrähe) that had just fallen from its nest.

We knew from the forester that the bird's mother would never accept it again and that it would perish or be taken by a fox or bird of prey, so we took it with us and constructed a comfortable cage for the tiny bird. Our feeding efforts with worms, caterpillars, tadpoles and so on were successful. The bird grew more and more and became very attached to us. Even our dachshund, at first a bit jealous, became used to this strange new member of the household. We named the rook "Jakob" and it accompanied us everywhere sitting on the shoulder and sometimes nibbling at one earlobe, a sign of affection. We tried to teach him to speak words, but "Jakob" just managed to repeat its own name. Finally, when our companion had reached maturity, it left us in search of a partner in the rook community.

Popular for a time was the breeding of the funny little white mice. Unfortunately ours were soon killed by a weasel.

Next we managed to catch a couple of dormice, lovely animals living in hollow trees. They resemble small squirrels a little bit and are only active at night. They are hibernating animals and are extremely shy (unsociable), and for this reason just a few people have seen them. As these droll animals created much noise in the night that prevented us and our dachshund to sleep, we took them back to their original living quarters at the fringe of the forest but only after having shown them proudly to the schoolmaster and our schoolmates.

When snow in winter was sufficiently high and had the right consistency we made a big snowman. The nose was the usual carrot or a yellow turnip; for eyes and buttons we took chestnuts, and mouth and ears were carbonized pieces of wood. When no discarded top hat or similar was available we placed a corroded bucket on his head. Finally he got a birch broom at his side.
We also had a lot of fun constructing "igloos" like the snow

houses of the Eskimos with hard-pressed snow blocks and small windows made of real ice plates cut out with my foxtail saw.

My brother used to chaff me because of an old woman I took pity on. Mrs. G. had escaped from the German-speaking part Bohemia of the former Czechoslovakia. She had lost all her relatives and belongings and had managed to reach the West and had been sent to our village. As she had no means and was too fragile to work, the community took care of her. She had been provided with a very small attic room above one of the public houses. As she needed some help I supplied her with firewood, got milk from the farmer and bread from the baker. As she could not see well I read aloud to her articles from the newspapers, short stories from books and passages from the Bible as she was unfit to walk the long way to the church at the other side of the village. Before Christmas I organized a small fir tree from the forest and decorated it with simple means. The nice old woman passed away before long and got a burial for the poor like so many in that turbulent times.

On "Father's Day" all male adults started in groups for an extensive excursion into the surrounding countryside. The shoulder bag contained some provisions such as bread, hard-boiled eggs and the inevitable bottle of "Hardenberger Korn" (a local brandy made of grain) or home-distilled potato spirit. Some singing songs, directed their steps to one of the popular taverns in the valley of the "Garte" creek or on the other side of the mountain in the valley of the "Lutter" creek. Some could not remember later how they had found their way back home, having been completely intoxicated. Others regained their balance after having slept over their drunken fit in a barn or in one of the sheds at the paddocks. Boozing was a widespread custom of the natives. The immigrant refugees had bigger problems to take care of and therefore a stronger reason to drown their sorrows in alcohol, but they were less affected for a simple reason: they had no cash or items to exchange for the bottled "soul comforter". For exactly the same reason they rarely frequented the public houses and taverns (Gaststätten). Later, when the equipment for fermentation was available, they took a sip once in a while from their precious small quantities of red currant, rhubarb, dandelion and elder flower wine of low-degree alcohol. In our village were some antisocial elements who invested most of their wages in spirits and used to give their women a regular dressing down. The neighbors and the pastor had to interfere.

The cabinet maker S., who had supplied me with leftover pieces of wood from his work to play with when I was smaller, allowed us to take away sawdust, which could be used for many things. In his dusty workshop we could watch how furniture and coffins were made and wooden spokes for wheels were replaced. Sometimes we could help him with simple tasks like planing a board or pasting assembled pieces of furniture. He loved to teach us something useful. I learned something about the treatment, the advantages and the beauty of the different kinds of wood. I liked the smell of the fresh-sawed boards. During this time just massive wood was used; the economical and much cheaper panels made of wood shavings and adhesive had not been invented and introduced yet. In this workshop we fixed up our first stilts. One has to be dexterous to walk with stilts. It was easy to get on them when sitting on an elevated place like the rear of a wagon or the platform, where every morning the farmers left their voluminous aluminum cans with fresh milk for collection by the dairy truck. Competition races with stilts took place and there were no few who got bloody noses or knees.

My brother was a bit older than me and was always ready for some tomfooleries. One summer day he and his companion Friedhelm were roaming around in an area down the village called "Winters Alpen". Both had climbed an old cherry tree and were busy enjoying the delicious fruit and stuffing them into their shirts for lack of bags. Unobserved, the owner of the orchard W. had come and placed himself equipped with a cudgel underneath waiting for both impatiently to teach them a lesson. Strategically and perfectly coordinated, the surprised ones let themselves with one accord suddenly fall down. The farmer not having counted on such a cleverly planned action was unable to catch the escaping boys with their loot. Mum, however, having with pleasure received the booty sensed somehow that a "thunderstorm" was approaching and got the story. To avoid trouble, she sent both boys to farmer W. to fetch some milk. Meanwhile W. had returned and was busy in the courtyard of his place seeming not to take any notice of them. After having received the milk from the farmer's wife the boys assembled all their courage and approached him from behind shouting, "Here we are!" In the meantime the farmer had calmed down, turned around and told them, "I think, I was like you when I was young! ... I do hope you will enjoy the cherries! ... Fruits from the neighbor's garden are still the best ones!" And turning to my brother he said, "And don't forget to give my best regards to your mother!" And with that the small event was soon forgotten.

It was spring 1948 when I was sent to the local school for the first time. I got the traditional "Schultüte" like all the other beginners. It was a long, conical, multicolored cardboard container filled with sweets and resembling the "fortunes cornucopia". I was very proud about my used old-fashioned leather satchel my mum had received from a helpful fellow villager. My schoolbooks were printed on yellowish low-quality paper and fell apart easily, but had to be returned at the end of the school year. The most important working utensil was the already-mentioned wood- framed slate with slater and a sponge hanging on a string. The slate had engraved lines on its front for writing letters and words and checkered ones for numbers and calculating on its rear. We learned still both ways of writing, first the former German letters (Sütterlinschrift) of the parents' generation and the present Latin alphabet. Most people nowadays are lost when confronted with the problem of deciphering old handwritten documents.

The absolute shortage of teachers caused by victims of the war, missing persons, POWs still in Siberia/Russia and those dismissed from school service because of their NS-party membership and activities had created a situation where it was common for classes of different levels in the elementary school to be instructed in one and the same classroom. The pupils who were actually being taught were sitting in the front rows and the remaining three classes in the rear were given writing or reading duties to keep them busy. Under those strange conditions the teacher could only handle the situation by means of a hazel rod, a ruler and slaps in the face. Down with the trousers and a powerful massage on the backside was the only way to maintain discipline. For one year my brother Wolf and I were sitting in the same classroom! When the schoolmaster had to leave the room for a while all hell broke loose. Dried peas were shot with blowpipes (pea shooters) or paper U-bolts were released with rubber rings. Pupils kicked at each other legs and ears and hair were pulled, especially the pig tails of the girls, but as soon as we could hear the creaking of the outer door and its shutting sound suddenly deathly silence prevailed and all bowed their heads over the slates, copy- and exercise books, pretending to be very assiduous and concentrated on their subject of instruction. When the schoolmaster was however absent for a longer period for going to the post office, to meet the mayor or for joining one of the scarce "Schlachtfeste" (pig slaughters), he appointed the most dominant and generally accepted pupil – it was of course always an older one – to oversee the classes. For the time of his absence he gave us an adequate writing work to do. Those who did not finish it to his full satisfaction were kept behind after school was over. That was embarrassing and unpleasant when there was fine playing weather.

The school benches had no back rests, forcing us to stay awake during the lessons. Underneath the desk was a shelf for the books and a hook at its side for the satchel. On the top was an even section with a recess for placing the slate pen, lead pencil, pen holder, sharpener and eraser, and next to it a square recess with an ink bottle and a metal cover. It was a really practical, functional and sturdy piece of furniture, which had in this form proved its worth for centuries. The slanting desktop and the massive benches were covered with the carved names of generations of pupils.

Stored in a huge locker beside the blackboard were the necessary utensils for teaching like books, chalk, maps, ink, ruler, sponge, disciplinary instruments and a bottle of spirit for the schoolmaster to fortify his nerves from time to time. The use of chalk must have been enormous because we dared to use it in many other ways. It was the pupil's job to keep the classroom clean by means of a broom, shovel, bucket, scrubber and cleaning rag, and a towel and sponge for the windows. Often those got the privilege for this job who had gotten into mischief. A birch broom was stored in the "Rumpelkammer" (lumber room) for cleaning the dusty area in front of the school. During the main break at around 10:30 a.m. we used to play football. As goal we used two logs from the pile of firewood, stored at the side of the school to feed the furnace in the winter season. An empty tin can served as football. When the "little ones" also got the chance to play, I was always condemned to be the goalkeeper. Because of my squinting I never managed to hit the can exactly in its center. This frustrating experience is perhaps the reason that I was never enthused about this game; that does not of course mean that I was not sportive. I was good in athletics and many years later I got some school awards and the official German sports badge.

A burly and well-fed boy used to tease us poorly dressed and undernourished children from the German Far East. On one of those occasions during the school break this guy had my brash brother in a “Schwitzkasten” (headlock), a painful form to immobilize an adversary. I liberated him from this uncomfortable and painful situation by tearing a nail-starring loose lattice from the “two-by-four” fence of the pastor’s orchard and started to hit the back of the offender, who was so shocked that he let my brother go and rushed home to see that his blood-covered back was taken care of. That small action got me, the “Schielbock” (squinting buck) some extra points especially from my brother, who always seemed to enjoy tormenting me.

Our first teacher was nicknamed “Igelvater” (father hedgehog) because of his brush-like spreading white hair. A girl happened to slip out this nickname during a lesson, but he was not angry; he gave a friendly reply: “... and you are my little hedgehog children!” He just taught us during the first year and went, I think, into retirement. His successor was tall, gaunt and used to take a little sip from the bottle of spirit from time to time. He was very proficient and did not just teach. On Sunday mornings he played the organ in our church or led the church choir, he directed the local choral society, organized festive processions, prepared small theater shows of the school children and grown-ups as well as poetry recitals for special occasions like jubilees. He took care of simple sports practices and kept alive the local traditions. To top it, he was an active member of the village council and of the “Skatrunde” (German card game) at the table of the circle of cronies in our tavern “Zum schwarzen Bären” (Black Bear). One should imagine: Four classes in one room, mastering of several teaching subjects and countless other activities and responsibilities! Those schoolmasters in the countryside, often looked down on, were often extraordinary personalities and universal talents, who “did the most with nothing”! They are the ones who deserve a monument. In our present pedagogical system we got of course another situation, but the teachers are more or less specialists in one or two subjects only.

The schoolmaster took us outside into the natural countryside and ordered us to draw a certain tree, flower or landscape with the grazing cattle or horses. In the village it was the church or one of the better-looking framework houses and their environs. He taught us many folk songs we had to sing during our “Wanderungen” (hiking tours) into the closer or more distant regions. He told us much about the local history and happenings in the past, the topography, the people, traditions and the nature with its animals and plants.

A few years later he was suddenly transferred to another faraway community for disciplinary reasons. It happened like this: While playing cards at the regular circle in the pub he had taken too much to the bottle. Unable to find his way home his fellow players, who had also taken a glass too much, had dropped him into a wheelbarrow used for carrying manure, driven him home and dumped him in front of his house entrance. The news of this happening had somehow reached the ears of the superiors at the education department in the city and was considered as an incident not appropriate for the dignity of the pedagogical fraternity. Subsequently the village lost probably the most versatile and active teacher it ever had.

By chance, about forty years later I got his address and went to pay him a visit together with my South Korean wife. He must have been over ninety, but he was healthy and full of spirit, still playing the organ in the church and an active member of the local glee club. To the acquaintances and friends we met my charming wife was presented as his lotus flower and I the most attentive pupil he ever had, which was of course not true. At that occasion I told him a story of our common time in the village school that made him double up with laughter. The following had happened: Adjacent to our garden, just separated by a barbed-wire fence, Schoolmaster B. owned an orchard. A magnificent old cherry tree stood in its middle. At picking time, while mum was away, I could not resist the temptation and climbed over the fence to collect a bucket full of the delicious black fruit in spite of the due respect I had for my teacher. By negligence it happened that I lost my only leather belt, while I was busy climbing through the branches of the tree. Shortly after the schoolmaster came accompanied by his wife and daughter to collect the ripe cherries, but they did not find so many anymore, instead, my fortunately unmarked lost belt, a very precious object for me. The next day in class B. displayed the belt in front of all the pupils and told us with an air of innocence that he had just found it and that he wanted to give it back to its owner. I offered no comment on this and concealed my blushing face sedulously in my schoolbook. My negligence and stupidity should not be cause for losing my face in front of the whole assembled classes. I knew exactly what awaited me in the case that I raised my hand ... a thorough thrashing with my proper belt. The fact that the teacher kept the belt frustrated me for a while, but "time is the best healer"!

One of the classmates of my brother Wolf was for that time of exotic origin. His nickname was "Kieke" (an abbreviation of "Enrique" – that is Spanish and means "Henry" in English). In the extended area of influence of Germany during the war the people had a lot of contact with foreigners and a mental image of nations underneath our "umbrella". Spain and Portugal, however, were neutral nations and far away at the southwestern corner of Europe.

How did it happen, that "Kieke's" family came to our village of all places? Like us they had by chance been allocated to our place by the authorities in charge, which were working with precision even in the prevailing chaos. They came from Berlin, where they had been bombed out of. So it happened that the population all over Germany had to move closer together to make room for the unfortunate millions of people who had lost the "roof over their head" including those who had lost their native land. I just remember that "Kieke's" father, a jeweler, had moved to Germany together with his family shortly before the start of World War II. They never talked about it, but probably they were victims of the Civil War that had raged in Spain from 1936 onward. The legal government together with the leftist "People's Front" supported by the Soviet Union and volunteers from all over Europe and overseas had fought three years against the insurgents, the rightist "Falange", that were supported by the Italian fascists and Nazi Germany. After the victory of the rightist Franco army many adherents and sympathizers of the losers had fled abroad. The family had already at the end of 1944 moved into a provisory accommodation in a farmhouse but had returned already at the start of the 1950s to their native land Catalonia in northeastern Spain. The letter with the many exotic stamps we received some time or other from Barcelona was a sensation and passed through the hands of countless curious villagers. Spain was at this time still a country beyond reach for the mass of the people.

American relief organizations, especially religious sects like the "Quaker Society of Friends", started, after some hesitation caused by the holocaust disclosures, to take care of the undernourished children of the refugees in the Bi-Zone (joined American- and British-occupation areas). One day at school break aluminum bowls with a handle and a spoon were distributed to us. We could keep them but were ordered to bring both items to school every day. From now on at break time a big cauldron filled with steaming thick rice soup and with changing garnishing was ready for distribution prepared by the teacher's wife. We each got a bowl full and those in special need got a supplementary portion if something was left over. We were greeting the distribution by drumming with our spoons onto the bottom of the bowls while singing, "We are hungry, we are starving, we have not yet got anything today!" ("Wir haben Hunger, wir haben Hunger ... Wir haben den ganzen Tag noch nichts gehabt!") At times we got also white bread with peanut butter, something never tried before.

My mother received one of those famous "Care" parcels supplied to families in need. They contained polished cans with cunningly designed practical opening devices containing real coffee, corned beef, egg powder, processed cheese, baking powder, flour, block- or liquid chocolate, cocoa, raisins and pudding powder so far as I remember, and all were considered treasures. Decades later we Western Germans were sending similar parcels in private initiative to people in need in Eastern Germany. Finally we had again mail contact with our grandaunt (my father's side) in New York. "Belle" was the widow of one of our emigrated granduncles. She came originally from the British colony of Jamaica in the Caribbean Sea. She took the trouble to send my grandmother some parcels for distribution in the family. One was especially for us and contained fitting used but first-class garment that smelled very good, coming directly from a dry cleaning. I tried on my first proper suit and was very proud when I had the opportunity to wear it the first time in public. In a small hidden inner jacket pocket I discovered a 1 US$ greenback. The cleaning staff must have overlooked it or Auntie Belle had slipped in inside afterward. Anyway, this precious bill with the picture of President General George Washington was not exchanged (1 US$ was 4,20 DM that time) but was kept as my talisman and went from hand to hand. Curious as I was I tried to find out everything about this fighter for the American independence and was at the end so well informed that I knew even more about that subject than our schoolmaster B.

Besides Uncle Axel the ethnologist and Pastor S., the forester E. and his daughter Rosemarie were excellent sources of information. The forester kept a dachshund who had become a companion of our dachshund Zumper. It was obvious that the human beings that went with them became friends too. His library, decorated with stuffed heads of wild animals like wild boar, red deer and birds of prey, antlers and furs, contained rows of bookshelves stuffed with old hunting magazines, encyclopedias, professional and general literature. When I started to read I borrowed from Rosemarie children's books of famous authors writing in German like Spieri, Busch, Hauff, Grimm, Rossegger, Löns, Thoma and Andersen; then I changed to international authors like Stevenson, Twain, May, La Fontaine, Dickens, Dumas until we moved to the city and I became a member of the public library where I could get more voluminous books. Just when I started to learn reading and writing my other grandmother, Hitta, started for lack of children's books to write for me the most common fairy tales by heart into simple copy books and decorated it with nice pencil drawings.

A relative of Mrs. von G., a spinster of about seventy years, Miss von H., or better, "Auntie Eva", living in the city turned up regularly at our place long after my playmate Erdmann and his mother and grandmother had moved away, to get a "bite" to eat. Bite is a little bit exaggerated because she had an artificial set of teeth that used to wander around in her mouth when speaking fast and emotionally and the denture had to be adjusted discreetly from time to time. She was an outspoken eccentric. She also came from our native land Silesia, and that was reason enough for the good soul to stick with my mother. She belonged to that generation of the Prussian landed aristocracy, who had irrevocable moral principles. In those circles the unmarried aunts used to live at the estates and castles of their brothers or other relatives, and they were no burden. At the giant dining tables were always served numerous guests and employees; for that reason there was always plenty prepared, and one person more or less did not count. The unmarried older ladies had, while their parents were still alive, enjoyed an excellent however one-sided education. That was done by private tutors, sometimes even foreigners at home. The landholdings of the nobility of the "German Far East" were in the majority far away from cities and high schools; that explains this system. My mother's excellent French was the result of the efforts of a French demoiselle who was employed as a tutor for my mother and her younger sister. There was of course also a music instructor. Contrary to present days much music was practiced at home. Those who choose or were selected to make a final examination at the "Gymnasium" (high school) or wanted to get a diploma in domestic science were sent to an appropriate boarding school. There the "young flowers of society" were drilled in the strict Prussian tradition for their later assignments. The famous boarding schools were, as a rule, former monasteries. The protestant "mother superior" governed there with draconian strictness over her protégées together with a selected teaching staff of outstanding quality. Those educational establishments possessed names like "Gnadenberg" (mountain of grace) or "Heiligengrabe" (holy grave) and had a resemblance to cadet colleges – just the military equipment was missing. My mother had studied at such institutions.

Auntie Eva, however, belonged to those ladies who had never seen such an institution from the inside. She was simply a part of the family – a little bit cranky, but never mind. Those often whimsical old maids were busy with reading, playing the piano, writing poems, embroidering, rose keeping, painting and drawing, playing bridge or chess and, most of all, keeping contact with the whole family clan by correspondence. Some of the more courageous ones enjoyed traveling. I was shocked when I discovered that Auntie Eva was incapable of repairing an open seam or sewing a loose button to her jacket; she begged my mother to do it. When still at home at their estates those ladies did not dare to be in the way of the room servants or the cook. From the financial point of view most of them had no problems. They got a small inheritance or an "Apanage" (compensation). There is a well-known phrase known in those circles to describe the situation of those beloved old aunties: "They came for a night's visit and stayed for the rest of their life!" For this group of susceptible and unpractical refugees the flight from their protected small world was a double catastrophe. They were confronted with a situation they were incapable of handling. With their principles they also did not want to be a burden to anybody. To earn some pennies, Auntie Eva drew pretty pictures, made portraits and cut silhouettes from black paper but had difficulty in finding customers for her works of art. People had other problems to deal with – art was not on the agenda. Then she earned some pocket money in elementary schools in villages around Goettingen telling fairy-tales and other interesting stories. The schoolchildren adored her and always begged her to continue her stories over the conceded time. She had an impressive way of presenting her stories, and I think she would have been a successful dramatic adviser in another life.

She was equipped with a sturdy walking stick and had high-laced walking boots and a huge black slouch hat. She announced her coming always with a postcard and we went to meet her at the railway stop of the neighboring community. My brother and I had to let her have alternatively our bed and we slept on straw sacks. We were not enthused about that at the beginning, because she always stayed a couple of days. She took us for long walks and explained to us many things about flora and fauna intermingled with stories from her beloved native land in the East. From time to time she stopped to draw with quick movements a pretty flower, a butter fly, a crippled tree or a bird on her sketching block she carried always in her shoulder bag. Her drawings and water colors decorated the walls of our home as well as our "guest book", where each guest was obliged to make an entry before leaving.

One day Lindau our "village-herald" (town crier) went on his way through the village swinging his handbell and announcing the incredible news that a cinema performance would take place in the other public house, the first one after the war. The projectionist arrived with a rickety three-wheeled van and started to prepare his projector on an elevated table at the rear of the hall. Two loudspeakers were installed and a large bedsheet was suspended from the ceiling of the stage. After the spectators had been warned not to step onto the electrical lines the lights were switched off and the preview with the news started: There were reports of the Berlin airlift; Formosa and the marshal Chiang Kai-shek and his communist opponent Mao Tse-tung; about POWs and their arrival at the reception camp Friedland, Germany; and about the politicians Schumacher and Adenauer. There were pictures of skyscrapers in New York, marching troops of the French foreign legion and of refugees in India. Pastor S. and other adults were treated with uncountable questions later on, to explain exactly the ins and outs of the matter seen in the news. Then the main movie started. There was no advertising yet ... "No hard cash, no consumers, no products!" It was an old German movie with Heinz Rühmann, still a production from the Goebbels era, who was minister of propaganda and took care that many superficial entertainment movies where made to distract the people in wartime from their problems. The movie was considered harmless and unpolitical and was admitted to be shown by the authorities. Its title was "Quax der Bruchpilot" (*Quax the Crash Pilot*), a really funny piece; we enjoyed the performance enormously.

Radio entertainment came much later. My mum had exchanged some items from the United States for an old "Braun Volksempfänger" (Braun people's receiver), a cheap mass-produced radio from the NS period. We could not use it for a long time because there was no way to get a power connection for our hut. The *Quax* movie had led us to build different types of aircraft from printed paper patterns, which had to be cut out with scissors and glued together according to instructions. With Friedhelm our hobby genius we started to construct model gliders that could really fly. My granny Hitta had sent me a fretsaw for my birthday with a packet of spare blades, an absolute requirement for such kinds of handicraft. The transverse frame of the wings and the fuselage made of very light balsa wood was in an improvised way covered with water-proof paper. The cabinet maker supplied the glue.

The first movie session was followed by others in more frequent intervals. The first foreign production was a soundless one – *Modern Times* – with Charlie Chaplin, and it made a deep impression on all of us. The dusty hall was always overbooked. Many people had to stand and seats were taken in turns to make everybody happy. During the war and before there had been shown just a few propaganda movies so one can sympathize with the immense enthusiasm of the people for this diversion.

Another sensation was the first brand-new car of the large-scale farmer W. H. It was an "Opel Olympia". It was actually an American car produced in a German factory by General Motors, but in wartime it had produced trucks and limousines for the German Wehrmacht. International business ... strange world! I was very impressed by the emblem: it was a geographical globe. The factory new limousine, a cabriolet smelt so well of fresh paint. One day W. H. picked me up on the road to the neighboring village, where I wanted to take a bath in the natural swimming pool, and gave me a lift.

There is still something to tell about this vivacious farmer. He loved hunting and owned a solid shooting lodge hidden deep in the forest above the village. He did not just chase hares and red deer but also attractive young ladies, mostly students from the university who succumbed to his rough charms. He used to invite them to watch animals and for a wholesome picnic in his hunting domicile and took the opportunity "to pick the flower". His haunted wife knew about his occasional escapades but remained composed because he always managed to act discreetly and to "keep it out of the news". Heino his son was also fond of the girls, but having a transport problem he had to be content with the young girls who helped out at harvest time.

Besides in the church choir and the the glee club, the population used to sing a lot just for entertainment when sitting at the spinning wheel still used at that time and while doing boring jobs like sorting dried peas and beans and doing the laundry, on excursions and on the fields during harvest time. I can still remember some of the folk songs, popular songs and hits of that time, like "Heideröschen" (Rose of the heath), "Am Brunnen vor dem Tore" (At the well in front of the village), "Barbara, Barbara komm mit mir nach Afrika" (Barbara come with me to Africa) and many others.

Later, more current ones from the radio and new movies were introduced. Some were really stupid, and we "composed" a couple of such nonsense songs ourselves. A popular one went like this : "Ein Affenopa sitzt am Fluss und angelt nach der Kokusnuss ..." (A monkey-grandfather is sitting at the river-bank fishing for coconuts ...).

Our mother "Maritta" was able to play a few musical instruments, but at first she got a "Hohner" mouth organ followed by an accordion. She knew already to play it but had not had the chance to practice it for a couple of years. Soon she achieved such a virtuosity that she was invited to play at family festivities to entertain the guests. She was an "all-round talent" and very practical, able to use hammer, nail, screwdriver, axe and saw.

If her carefully maintained bicycle had a problem or a puncture she took care of it herself. She even got a driver's license, for women not very common at her time. At home in Silesia she often used my father's car to take care of shopping or other matters in the city, to see her mother-in-law, her parents or other relatives and friends. In the war the car was confiscated by the armed forces like most of the civilian limousines. It took well over a decade until she had the opportunity to drive one of my first cars. Even later, when she could have managed financially to own a small car, she resisted and preferred to take the train and taxi. Driving on our present streets and highways was a bit too stressful for her.

When conditions after the introduction of the Deutsche Mark were slowly improving and the travel limitations were lifted, we went to visit our grandparents in Buedingen, Hesse state quite often, especially in the summer holidays. Grandmother's nickname Hitta was the abbreviation of Maritta and again a shorter form of her real name "Margarethe". In our family clan nicknames were so common that in most cases we did not know the real given name of a person – it was never used except in official documents. Another problem was that we often had up to seven given names as did I and my brother, all names of godfathers, uncles, ancestors and so on. My wife now makes a joke about this calling us walking "tombstones", because the people who gave us their names are long since dead.

A lot could be told about "Villa Alfred" and its people, but I will restrain myself and concentrate on matters important for a child of my age at that time. Just to get a picture: My grandparents had been received as refugees with an unusual kindheartedness and understanding by Prince Dieter von Y., who was married to the cousin of my mother, my godmother Auntie Sieglinde.

The attic of the villa was a fantastic playground for a child of my age. It was crammed with dusty lumber and junk-like furniture, lockers and boxes full of old-fashioned dresses, hats, helmets, uniforms, toys, books, pictures and much more. The exotic stuff was covered with dust, spider webs and bird droppings. In a chest I discovered an old-fashioned phonograph (gramophone) that had to be wound up by means of a crank handle. It was accompanied by a selection of shellac records with needles. A new world was opened for me, another musical dimension, that of the operas. For hours I could listen to the melodies of "His Master's Voice" records like "The barber of Sevilla/Carmen/The Gipsy Baron/The nutcracker/Hoffmanns's Tales/The abduction from the Serail" and countless other compositions from Strauss/ Smetana/Stravinski/Verdi/Mozart and so on, which enriched my limited repertoire. Popular melodies of the "Golden Twenties" and the 1930s were existing too. I remember Richard Tauber with his unforgettable piercing tenor voice singing "Das ist der schönste Tag in meinem Leben ..." (That is the most beautiful day in my life ...). Names like Enrico Caruso, Beniamino Gigli and Arturo Toscanini belonged to my heart from now on.

My grandfather was a good-natured and warm-hearted personality and a passionate dog fancier. The dogs of the area got this message very fast, especially those without a master, the stray dogs. An American tank unit was stationed in Buedingen at this time. When the GIs or officers of those barracks were called back to the United States or were transferred to another base abroad, they did not know what to do with their dogs and let them simply free somewhere. A couple of them found their way to my grandfather and he took good care of them. On one visit I found that my grandfather had seven dogs of different breeds in his care. He was walking all of them on the leash like a noisy family at least twice a day in the close-by park of the castle and on the adjacent pastures. He and his dog circus were a common and strange sight. If you wanted to take a seat in one of the comfortable seasoned leather armchairs in the living room of the villa you could be sure that they were already occupied by the animals that populated the place. With the greatest reluctance they gave up their throne or even had to be removed by force.

In the villa was a large room called the “Waffensaal” (arsenal). It contained a collection of medieval and, later, rare weapons displayed hanging on or standing against the walls. There were original knight’s panoplies, swords, “morning stars” (clubs with iron spikes), flintlock muskets and needle guns. When it was raining and we had to stay inside I was permitted to assist when the objects were cleaned once in a while by “Tralla” (the nickname of my grandfather). One of those flintlocks had attracted my attention because of its beautiful shape and its decorative chase work. One morning “Tralla” went to one of his cronies, who owned the local pharmacy, to get all the ingredients to prepare the traditional gunpowder reinvented by Berthold Schwarz, a monk, as he explained to me, and I learned that the name of “Schwarzpulver” (black powder) came from the monk’s name and not from its color. The ingredients are saltpeter (potassium nitrate), sulfur and charcoal powder. To handle this gunpowder is not dangerous as long as it kept away from fire. The three materials have to be mixed in an exact proportion to each other. After having finished the job and the powder had been stored away safely, he demonstrated how to prepare ball shots. Lead was molten directly over the embers of a coal fire and filled into a hollow casting mold. The roughness of the balls were then removed with fine emery paper and were polished. We went into the vast garden to train shooting from a distance on a paper he had fixed on the enclosing stone wall. I kept the dented musket balls for a long time as souvenirs. The weapons still exist and some are displayed now on the “Ronneburg”, a fortified medieval castle near Buedingen.

Back home in our community they were just busy to repair the long macadam road “Neue Weg” (New Way) that lead from the eastern end of the village up into the forest in order to facilitate the transport of tree trunks by the lumberjacks. That gave us the idea of constructing a "soap-box chariot". It was a really simple contraption: A wide and sturdy board served as chassis. Transverse-wise underneath at the rear we fixed a square timber with long nails and those which jutted out from the board were hammered flat. On this timber we fixed the axle of a discarded perambulator or other means of transport using U-bolts and screws. At the front we did the same, but this time the axle-bearing timber was not nailed to the board. Instead, we drilled a hole through the middle of both the board and the timber and placed a bolt with a wide head and large-distance washers there and fixed it loosely with a nut and counter nut so that the timber could move easily. Steering was done with two straps fixed at both sides of the transverse timber. After the wheels had been placed on the axles we applied two levers beside the rear wheels, which were either pressed against the wheels or on the ground for braking. Finally, a sack with straw for seating was placed on the board and strapped tight. On a later improved model or, better, "bone shaker", we used the handlebar of a bicycle for steering. We could not drive this devil's contraption alone; one had to steer it with the reins like a horse and the copilot sitting at the rear was in charge of the brakes racing down the way. I admit that this primitive four-wheeler was not something to be registered at the patent office, but it worked. We enjoyed feeling like race drivers.

In winter the boys used something much more sophisticated that had skids instead of wheels: a bobsleigh. It even had railings at its side to hold on and a real steering wheel. It belonged to a group of senior boys who had constructed it and offered place for about six persons. The skids had a metal sheathing and braking was done with hooked levers pressing on the ground. The steering wheel was taken from a former British army truck that had been shot to pieces in the last days of the war and had been since then corroded in one of the stone quarries not far away.

Unfortunately, the bob hit a telegraph pole and the boy steering it suffered a serious fracture at the base of his skull and had to spend some weeks in the hospital. The surgeon fitted a silver plate over the damage to the skull. It is the only noteworthy accident in the village I can remember.

Talking about this I have to mention our indefatigable country Dr. N., a general practitioner who had his office in the village next to ours. He was one of those helpful experienced representatives of his profession, who, not minding wind and weather, nights and weekends, took care of his rural patients even at home if necessary, coming at first by bike and horse wagon. He treated his patients still with conservative means when pharmaceutical products were unavailable. My brother and I were ordered to take regularly twice a day cod-liver oil, which had a repulsive smell but a strengthening property. The bad cold I attracted when I broke through the ice of our fire-brigade pond was treated with his homemade cough cure. He was also willing to help a farmer when complications arose concerning the birth of calves and foals while his colleague the veterinarian was busy somewhere else or unavailable. Frequently the doctor was paid with natural produce and refugees were often treated free of charge.

At one of my later birthdays I got finally my long-yearned-for "Krachledernen" (Bavarian-style leather breeches and shorts). All my godparents and other relatives had contributed some hard cash to render possible the acquisition of this item made of buckskin. In the summertime my mother was from now on relieved from repeatedly patching up my thorn and shredded shorts or trousers. After having worn it for a long time it lost, to my regret, its original softness and became so stiff that I could stand it in the corner like a piece of furniture.

Our first camera was a black, box-shaped one from AGFA. There were no complicated preparations necessary to take a picture;

you just had to look through the viewer, hold it motionless and press the button. The pictures were accordingly of a very limited quality. On many pictures my mother took the heads or legs were missing, because she did not manage to keep the camera motionless when she pressed the button. We called them "Guillotine pictures". One of the first I still got shows our "palace" with the self-made rabbit hutch in the front and another with our loo and woodshed behind.

With the assistance of my mother a tiny garden was prepared for my own use. After some fiascos caused by indefatigable hard-working moles, who "helped" me to break up the soil, I was able to grow radish, salad and scarlet runner beans.

I was in need of a sturdy rope to construct a swing but could not manage to get one anywhere, and those in the stores for household articles in the city were too expensive. Finally I had a good idea. When harvesting the corn the sheaves were no longer bound with straw ropes but automatically with a sturdy string. Before threshing later on, those strings were simply slit open and wasted. I collected those masses of thrown-away cuttings and tied them together. A handful of what were now long strings were carefully interwoven like a pigtail to form a sturdy rope. That was fixed loop-like at two points of the thickest branch of the apple tree standing in front of our hut. At last I prepared a short seating board and carved a notch at each side, then the seat was placed into the loop and the swing was ready. Even grown-up people could use it. After a while the improvised rope scoured through at its fixing points but that was no problem as I got enough rope in reserve to replace it. Next I made a rope ladder and also used the same material for a hammock.

Finally I "inherited" from the daughter of the pub owner a pair of metal-frame spectacles she had outgrown. It was, however, a disadvantage that I broke the frame continually during my venturesome daily life, especially while climbing trees. Our village plumber Heinz G. who was married to Antonia, a pretty Ukrainian former D. P., repaired the wire like frame so often that it was of course covered with countless soft solder spots. I often forgot or lost the eyeglasses somewhere, but they were always like magic returned to me. Everybody seemed to know to whom this strange object repaired dozens of times belonged to. After my second, and this time successful, eye operation at the university hospital in Goettingen my mother could afford to get a new pair of horn-rimmed eyeglasses for me. On this occasion I got also my first sturdy rubber boots with profile soles.

The next problem on the agenda to be taken care of was my stammering. In the meantime the city could now be reached by postbus, so it was possible to send me to regular sessions to the "HNO" (otorhinolaryngology) department of the university to get a speech training. When I think about it now, it reminds me of the training "Eliza Doolittle", the rubbish collector's daughter, received in the play *My Fair Lady* by George B. Shaw. Like her I had to repeat the strangest combinations of words and sounds again and again. Anyway, it was quite successful.

My teeth had to be straightened too. A special, ugly-looking device, a pink plastic-wire construction was made to measure in the laboratory of our dentist Dr. K. to fit my upper palate and row of irregular teeth. It was necessary to adjust the instrument at intervals by means of a screw to maintain the tension on the teeth. It was extremely vexing to carry this nasty instrument of torture. When it hurt too much I took it out and slipped it into the pockets of my trouser ... the loosing of the instrument was preprogrammed. Once I was searching for two days for this ugly but really important object. I was despondent about it but hid the matter from my mum. A weight was off my mind when I finally found it in the hayloft of farmer H.'s barn. My mother had already enough problems with my elder brother, who was sent to a boarding school in a place some 50 km away. Meanwhile she got a small war widows' and orphans' pension, but it hardly covered all expenditure.

Here is one of our many silly hobbledehoy tricks: To tease the villagers my friend R. and I used to hide behind a hedge at the most frequented street crossing in the upper village near the school. A discarded wallet or purse was visibly placed into the middle of the street connected with us by means of a fine string covered with dust. When a passer-by wanted to pick it up we pulled it towards us and had a lot of fun watching and hearing the surprised reaction of the different people. The most common remark was "Of course, again you good-for-nothings with your lousy pranks! You really need a rubdown!"

Our landlord was a part-time farmer. His regular job was a representative of an established insurance company.

From time to time he came to see us and check if everything was in order, in particular, the recently fresh tarred roof of our hut that used to leak before. I seem to have never seen him without one of his big cigars. The empty cigar boxes were reserved for me. They were perfect containers for my collection of bugs and other items like fossils, dried plants and leaves.

"Uncle Hermann" always called my mother "Mädchen" (girl). To call her with our family name appeared to him as too official and by her given name as importunate. His hearing was impaired and the conversations a bit noisy and strenuous. Once he explained to us in his thundering voice the reason for the existence of our hut: His best friend was the biggest timber dealer in the city and owner of a sawmill. To do him a favor he had erected the hut. It should have served as a passing emergency dwelling in case his friend was bombed out. As that had not happened we had been the last family at this moment to use it. He could not have imagined that it would be for years the improvised home for refugees after the war. The rent was very low, because there was neither electricity nor running water. Just shortly before we moved into the city, the hut was connected with the public power line and we could use our radio. Uncle Hermann told us a couple of farmer jokes in his heavy "Lower-Saxony" dialect. One of those I can still remember: "An insurance agent offers two insurances to a hesitating farmer, one against fire and one against hail and violent storms. After some time of reflection the farmer agrees to take the first one. Asked why not both he answers: 'I know how to start a fire, but I am incapable to let it hail!'" Uncle Hermann owned a seasoned giant nut tree. In autumn we were permitted to gather the fallen nuts. When he left he always slapped my mother benevolently on her well-proportioned behind. It was considered a fatherly compliment so my mother did not react indignantly. He was a typical original "Urgestein" (archetype) of the region.

Opposite the pastures that bordered our premises and close to the school a worker was living in a rickety small half-timbered house. He was the owner of a huge, black, unpredictable, fierce German shepherd dog that was always chained to his kennel. To make the dog offensive he incited it, unseen by the villagers, to chase the cattle on the pastures. One time, when I roamed around I observed that the furious dog had gotten its teeth into the flank of an angry bull that dragged him like that over the meadow, and when it finally let go it was chased by the bull with lowered horns until the dog escaped through the barbed wire fence. To my knowledge man and dog were never caught "in flagrante", otherwise he would have had a big problem. One day when passing the house of that brute on our way home accompanied as usual by our faithful wire-haired dachshund Zumper, the furious barking and chain-dragging shepherd dog contrived to tear itself off its chain and assail our little dog. Being a male one Zumper fought courageously but had no chance against this untamed beast. The dachshund was bitten to pieces. His lights and other entrails were damaged to a degree that he died soon after in his sleeping basket. We had lost a very close friend, a member of the family, who had been our watchful bodyguard in good and in bad times.

Soon the forester E. arranged that we got another thoroughbred male dachshund, again a wire-haired one but of light brown color. It was baptized Jockel and became soon the darling of the whole village. Contrary to his forerunner, who had been extremely distrustful towards strangers Jockel was indiscriminately friendly towards everybody, wagging his tail continuously. That should not obscure the fact that he had a hereditary sense for hunting. He loved to chase wild animals as soon as he was released from his leash and did not obey commands anymore, being absolutely concentrated on his target. It happened that he dragged stealthily already foul-smelling and disintegrating small game like hares, crows, partridges and so on through the open door and underneath our mother's bed. We became conscious of it because of the bestial offensive stench, something that is perfume for dogs. The animal otherwise so amiable used to defend its "five-star delicacy" ferociously and only with the assistance of a broom could we give the gourmand the sack.

By the way, Jockel avenged inadvertently the murder of his forerunner by killing some young ducklings of the owner of the shepherd dog. Both dogs were specialists in ferreting foxes out of their lairs by slipping in and chasing them out in hot pursuit. Jockel, however, was nearly asphyxiated on one occasion, when a courageous fox showed resistance and started to bury the dog by blocking the exits with soil. We guessed it, because neither the fox nor the dog appeared and there was no sound coming from the lair. We were making such a noise by shouting into the opening that the fox was so irritated that he left through another exit. Dirt-covered and visibly shocked by this dangerous experience and trembling all over, Jockel reappeared after a while, but it did not last long until his hunting instincts were revived. A couple of years later he unfortunately died of an embolism that was originally caused by a broken leg when hit by a passing car.

Our Villa Mud had an annex, a shack for storing firewood. For lack of storage space inside our hut we constructed some shelves there for the storage of sealed provisions like tinned food and preservation glasses. In winter those items were protected by straw and a thick horse blanket. It happened on an extremely cold January night that most of the glasses froze and cracked. After all the trouble of gathering and preserving those provisions we could of course not throw away the precious foodstuff. The fragments and splinters of glass were carefully gathered and sorted out, and for a while we were exclusively fed with these rescued vegetables and preserved fruit. We ate very, very carefully, like never before or since, in order not to damage our teeth or swallow one of those overlooked minuscule splinters of glass.

The village even had a small post office. It was "governed" by "Auntie Miele". As she was also in charge of delivering the mail, the office was just opened for a short period in the morning. In old documents I found a list of mail prices before 1948; here are some examples: a postcard was 0.12 RM, a printed matter up to 20 g 0.06 RM and a regular letter up to 20 g 0.24 RM. We always received a lot of mail, because "Bibi", our mum's nickname, was an eager correspondent. The nice old postwoman came for this reason regularly to our hut, took a rest and gave us news from the community and its environs. For me it was a pleasant distraction to help her in distributing the mail, which was not an easy matter for her with her heavy leather pouch when the roads and lanes were frozen or when the side lanes like ours turned into a quagmire when it rained. One day she informed us that we should pick up a parcel from her office. When we opened it, we found carefully wrapped two brand new petrol lamps a thoughtful friend had got for us. Reading was much more fun now. Even today when I get the smell of lamp oil in my nose it reminds me of comfortable evenings with absorbing literature in our lonely wooden "palace".

My grandma Hitta, who was so well-versed in sewing sawdust-filled dolls made from rags shortly after the war to earn some money, disposed of an unusual natural gift already known in her circles in our native land. She was very successful in healing exterior diseases with magic spells. I cannot explain it, but she had an overwhelming personality. When she came to visit us she offered her talents to help some villagers with medical problems. The mistrust was blown away when older people, who had suffered already for years, were completely healed within a short time. She was also occupied in telling the future from playing cards, the persons in question had to shuffle the cards themselves. We said jokingly that in medieval times she would have ended on a pyre burned as a sorceress.

The slaughter of pigs in the village was always a very important matter. When the time of the illegal "black" slaughtering was over, a deputy of the public health department was sent from the city to check the meat for trichina (*Trichinella spiralis*) before it was processed. With a microscope he appraised the innards and foremost the liver. When everything was according to the law, the show could go on. The pigs were normally killed by a quick and expert gash through the carotid artery. The collected blood was not wasted but collected to make "Blutwurst" (black pudding), a local specialty. The headless animal was then placed on a heavy hook fixed hanging from the ceiling or a beam, the innards were taken out and the pig was dissected. When tin cans for conservation were available again, meat boiled or in chunks or minced in different compositions was filled into the cans and sealed right away with a hand-operated appliance. The guts were thoroughly cleaned and used as skin for the different varieties of sausages. All the mixing took place in large wooden troughs. The different mixtures of meat, spices and salt were filled into the prepared guts. Those were closed with strings and hung into the curing room. For smoking of ham and sausages the shavings of beech wood were used. I just want to give a general idea of the procedure. Anyway a lot of work is involved before everything is processed, and then the best pieces of meat are prepared for a wholesome dinner.

Sometime or other my mother's younger sister, "Gi" (abbreviation of "Gisela"), came to see us and decided to stay in the area. Her fiancé had started agricultural training at a nearby state domain. Soon he struck up a friendship with farmer and pub-owner G. of the "Black Bear". In his free time he assisted him to cultivate the soil and at harvesting time when necessity arose. When my auntie married they got a live sucking-pig as a present from his friend and the privilege to leave it as a "pension guest" in the farmer's pigsty until it was fully grown, then to be transformed into sausages and other pork products. This became a long tradition and each member of the growing family was looking forward for the annually recurring "pork festival" that helped to support the supply of food for the later five-headed family. The tradition continued long after my uncle had finished his agricultural studies at the University of Goettingen and had a position as lecturer. It only ended when he was offered an academic chair in Berlin, which was a bit too far away.

The first bananas, oranges and lemons that were offered in our general store caused a sensation. Many people had heard about it but never seen them "in natura". A long queue was forming in front of the shop. Later roasted coffee beans appeared on the shelves in pretty tin boxes or cans. Most of the villagers had not tasted the "real stuff" for over fifteen years. The wonderfully smelling roasted beans were still ground to powder in the old wooden coffee mills that had over the years been used to grind something else and the molars had become blunt. But the greatest joy for mum was the good-smelling soap made of palm oil, which she had so long been without. The famous brand of washing powder, "Persil", was again available and facilitated the weekly laundry, but the washboard with its waved wood or metal surface and the zinc washing tub were still in use for a long time. Ration cards had been in use for over a decade as in England. According to one for the year 1946 my mother was entitled to 1,249 calories per day provided that she really got what was printed on those cards. Nowadays people are thinking of calories only when they are overweight!

The time of yellow turnips was over; that had been our main staple for some time. Concerning our illumination we still had to be happy with our petrol lamps and candle lights.

As already mentioned in another context, the narrow-gauge steam railway was a reliable and cheap means of public transport in good and bad times and had been taken to the heart of the people. The students' associations were still very numerous at that time and added some color to the university city. On "Father's Day" and Pentecost the "Gartetalbahn" (Garte-Valley-Train) was completely in the hands of the "alma mater". It was so crammed that even the footboards and the roofs of the carriages were occupied. Relay races were performed to compete with the running train. The students mostly won, no wonder, the maximum speed was limited to 20 km/h (12.5 mi/h). They also used artful tricks to slow down the train by lubricating some stretches of the tracks with soft soap or axle grease. Another hoax was to disconnect unobserved some carriages during a stop. The whole nonsense was taken with humor by the staff of the GTB Train Co. It was public relations and advertisement free of charge for the train and the scenic route. Destinations of those excursions were the "Eichenkrug" (oak-tree tavern), a typical German country pub on the slopes of the "Gleichen" mountains, where people took a rest before or after a hiking tour. Further on was the "Waterloo" (later renamed "Pigalle"), where the students could also dance, exactly what they liked. The "Brotzeit" (picnic) was often taken along in baskets by the thrifty female students, but in both establishments the beer was good and the simple menu fitted the small purse of the young "alma mater". The return ticket was 0.85 DM.

The city of Goettingen had used the former German air force base with its hangars, workshops and barracks to accommodate an intermediate school and a movie studio. Some of the first popular low-budget movies after the war were produced there. One with the title "Der tolle Bomberg" (*The Eccentric Bomberg*) with the famous German actor and shanty singer Hans Albers was created there after a best-seller story of that time. This movie made this steam railway line famous. The protagonist "Baron von Bomberg" stages in this movie a race between his horse-drawn equipage and the driver of the steam locomotive and wins, of course. The operation of this narrow gauge (750 mm) railway line, founded in 1896, ended during a nationwide rationalization initiative in 1959 to the regret of the entire population. Today it would be a profitable tourist attraction.

In the early years after the war the use of plastic materials of today's well-known artificial materials like PVC, Viscose, Acryl, Vinyl and so on was absolutely unknown. The "German Frauleins" in the big West German cities were happy about the pretty nylons they got as presents from the American GIs as compensation for their affection. Concerning plastic the world was still in waiting. Firewood was stored underneath tarred tarpaulins or corrugated iron sheets. Containers were made of metal, tin, glass, wood, clay, canvas or cardboard. Instead of plastic bags people used baskets, textile bags, string nets or the dear old rucksack for shopping. In the shops paper bags and sheets of newspaper were used for wrapping goods. The paper bags were often returned when empty for a second use. Even in the city milk was still sold loose, everybody had to get it in a milk can with a sturdy wooden handle. Refrigerators in private households did not exist yet; there were just some old iceboxes or ice cellars in the villages with blocks of ice from the wintertime. The farm houses often had vaulted cool cellars. The storage room was located at the cool northernmost corner of the house adjacent to the smoking/curing room where the sausages and ham were hung. Fine-meshed wire panels were used to keep away the many flies. In the kitchens were hanging those ugly brown sticky flycatchers. The methods of food conversation were adjusted to the situation. Easily perishable victuals were never stored in large quantities. You got only such an amount of vegetable from the garden that you could use immediately. Potatoes were a real problem as they started to sprout in late winter (today they are treated chemically to avoid this). Sauerkraut, a very healthy and becoming vegetable, and cucumbers were preserved in stoneware pots. Fruit was dried in the attic or in the oven. Certain kind of apples were stored on racks in the cool cellar for months but had to be turned from time to time. Mushrooms, beans peas, leaves for plant tea, herbs, garlic and so on were also dried in the attic and stored afterwards in airy bags and hung on the beams. Easily spoiled beef had to be consumed right away or had to be stored in the pickling vat.

The slaughtering festivals were an occasion where the villagers finally could enjoy some fresh meat after some time of forced abstention. For some strange reason the villagers did not care for fresh liver, so it was no problem to get some when an animal was slaughtered. I still like liver of all kind of animals. The mass production today, however, forces the farmers to treat their cattle with too many chemicals. Liver is a filter organ and nowadays contains a lot of chemical residues, so eating liver now is not so much fun anymore when you think about that!

Due to the missing foreign seasonings and the means of our present methods of conservation, especially deep freezing and fridge, the “rural cuisine” was rather modest. Everything had to be practical; there was no demand for “finesse” even after the “rainy days” of the 1940s. The season decided what was served for dinner! Because of the much better cooling conditions, slaughtering was preferably done in mid-winter.

The shortage of goods forced the people to be parsimonious and waste nothing. As result there was practically no waste. Leftovers from the kitchen were fed to the countless animals or composted, combustibles were burned together with the garden litter and the deadwood. The rest went to the metal collector Resebeck or into the abandoned stone quarries. To throw away a bottle was out of question; it was something precious. Even rags were used until they fell apart; they were of natural fabric and dissolved or burned easily. The giant “recycling problems” we have now with our civilization’s waste did not exist. There was no refuse-disposal service except in the cities!

The village had not been provided with an athletic ground. The farmers did not want to sacrifice a field or pasture ground in the fertile valley down the village. The parish council had repeated meetings in the “Black Bear” concerning this matter, and finally after the consumption of a lot of “Goettinger Beer” and “Hardenberger Spirit” somebody had an inspiration. Up the village opposite the forest existed a sloping stony area good for nothing, and that was the place where they decided to create a football field by excavating and refilling ground to create an even area. In the community’s treasury was as most of the time at a “low tide”. One of the elders with good connections managed to get an appointment with the commander of the British forces stationed in the Ziethen barracks in the city to ask him for help.

The commanding officer of the “Scottish Border Guards” (COSB) or “Highlanders” considered the whole matter as an opportunity of a practical engineering training for his men. One dry summer day he drew up with his heavy equipment and started to turn the area in question upside down. After just two or three days the heavy work was done and it remained for the community to wait until the topped-up ground had settled to finish the job. I heard that this sports ground still exists. It cost the community just some barrels of beer and a couple of wicker baskets full of "Mettwurst" (sausages), rolls and "Schmantekuchen" (cream cake) for the efficient and helpful "Tommies".

The heavy oaken beer barrels for both of the villages' "Gaststätten" (public houses) were delivered at this time on open horse wagons specially constructed for this trade. It was moved by "Hanoverians", powerful brewery-owned horses. The leather harnesses were decorated with polished brass fittings. The coachman could already be heard from far away cracking his whip to urge along the good-natured draft horses. It was quite a job, to unload those heavy, bulging barrels and to haul them through the two-winged flap down into the cellar storage. After it was done and the empty barrels had been loaded onto the wagon, the driver, who was always wearing a large leather apron and a black leather cap, got his obligatory well-earned "Humpen" (stoneware drinking mug) of pale ale. The daily consumption of beer of those thickset coachmen must have been enormous.

We made then our own whips from young ash trees, which were nicely decorated using my carving knife, and solicited the thin leather strips from the cobbler. He had an interesting workshop and was in a position to make crude laced working boots after leather was again available. In bad times the soles of the repaired shoes were fixed with wood pegs instead of studs. On his battered sewing machine he repaired everything made of leather or canvas.

My first "new" leather shoes mum acquired in a "Salamander" (shoe shop) in the city, then a famous brand in Germany. At that time they had a powerful smell of tannic acid and were equipped with straps and clasps instead of laces that would have soon torn or probably got lost. My thrifty mother always paid heed to small matters like this and tried to get the best quality when she could afford it. She had an aversion for "good looking junk". "Expensive is not expensive and cheap is not cheap" was one of her principles. I never forgot this. For a childish reason the name of "Salamander" is still in my mind. In that shoe shop I got a kind of comic book free of charge, a public relations gimmick of the shoe company. The hero of the picture story was the salamander (batrachian) "Lurch", who had countless adventures while wearing salamander shoes.

Easter, the beginning of the spring season, was traditionally celebrated in a special form. The inside of the church was decorated with fresh fir branches and fully packed, with many participants standing. Pastor S. resuscitated animated the "Holy Land" and the story of the Lord in the mind of the assembled congregation. I suppose that for practical reasons the villagers decided to celebrate weddings on Easter to reduce the expenditure. Easter was also an occasion to receive relatives and friends from the "outside world". In the evening the giant Easter Fire, a relic from the far Teutonic past, was started above the village. All members of the community had provided the fuel such as logs, broken boards, branches and other combustibles, but the original amount of firewood had been gathered in the forest by pupils and the candidates for confirmation under the guidance of the forester and the schoolmaster. Some reliable young men were ordered to take care of the disused wagon- and cartwheels that had been prepared with straw, rags, shredded tarred paper and so on. They were saturated with petroleum, set on fire and one by one released down the incline of the hill opposite of the village. It was a spectacular sight. As always at such festivals beer barrels were tapped and large quantities of "Hardenberger Korn" or potato "Schnaps" were consumed. The village's communist, his tongue loosened by alcohol, began to sing the "International", the national anthem of the SU and to abuse the western militarists, imperialists, war mongers, plutocrats and exploiters of the workers, all hirelings of the American capitalists. He proclaimed that the beloved father Stalin would take care of it and create a paradise for all toiling farmers and workers alike and that he would also complete the communist world revolution. We brothers were very impressed about his speech but did not trust him after having previously experienced the start of the communist regime in the Soviet-occupied zone. At the end of his dramatic appearance he was so "filled up" (intoxicated) that several men had to carry him home.

The conservatives of the village were a minority and reserved in their attitude. The tune was called by the supporters of "Ollenhauer", the leader of the formerly forbidden social democrats and of course the incorrigibles, whose remarks like "If Adolf (Hitler) would still be alive, he would teach them a lesson!" or "He would tell them on which side their bread is buttered!" were common, but disregarding a few politically motivated noisy arguments and brawls that took place in the public houses everything went smoothly and harmoniously in the interest of the community. The majority of the people wanted to have their peace and were not very interested in politics, having other more pressing problems to take care of.

On Easter Monday morning the young people left the village. They carried fresh eggs, lard, ham, melted fat, bread, frying pan, drinks and matches in their bags and knapsacks. Depending on the weather conditions they set out for shacks in the meadows, or to picturesque places at creeks, ponds or on mountain slopes further away from the village, where they started a small fire to prepare their fried eggs and the rest of the picnic. This was followed by songs, some entertainment and card games. "Eierbacken" (frying eggs) at Easter was an old tradition in Lower Saxony and nobody, not even the pastor, could tell me when and why it started. It also is probably a Teutonic ritual like the eviction of the witches with noisy firecrackers at New Year's Eve and the Easter Fire to welcome spring. In ancient Greece the egg and phallus were symbols of fertility in connection with the sowing of seeds in springtime. I am sure that our Teutonic-Germanic forefathers had similar conceptions. Anyway, the "Eierbacken" was something the young people liked a lot. Finally this was a festive occasion where they were among themselves without being patronized by adults.

Near the small hill "KrietersKopp" in the direction of the state domain, where we used to collect beech nuts for making oil in the early years, stood the giant so-called "1,000 jährige Buche" (1,000-year-old beech tree) surrounded by legend and myth. It was stupendous that such a tree could have survived all the storms of the centuries. Several kids had to join hands to encompass this relic from the past. I am sure that the tree could have told a lot of stories. Perhaps the ruling lord of the region had passed judgement there on offenders and some had been punished by hanging from the branches of this tree. The thirty years' religious war had once devastated these lands and whole villages had disappeared. Perhaps the marauding lansquenets had erected their tents around there and divided up their booty.

A little bit further in the South opposite the "Garte" (creek) valley were the "Gleichen", two equal mountain peaks close to each other (gleich = equal). In medieval times two fortified castles had been there, but they had been destroyed during wars. The stones had been used by people of the surrounding villages as building material for their houses and farms. Seen from far away the mountains resembled the breasts of a woman. Because of the wonderful view over the region from the top they are a favorite hiking destination. When I was very young I remember still the charcoal burners with their blackened faces working at their kilns in the forests surrounding these mountains.

Another destination for our excursions even further in the South was the "Hurkutstein". At that time many myths of the old German tribes and the medieval times were spread around, and one dealt with that rock. “Hurkut”, explained our schoolmaster B., signified something like “to hide and squat” in the old German language, and he told us the following story: On the landmark of the region the twin mountains “Gleichen” existed the two fortified castles of two brothers, the knights “von Gleichen”. It was arranged that the younger of those two brothers should inherit everything after the death of the older one, who was childless. To the greatest surprise of all concerned the wife of the older brother gave birth to a son and heir after decades of barrenness. The extremely disappointed younger brother pondered over it for a long, long time and thought out a scheme to get rid of the child. In modern mafia manner, perfidious as he was, he bribed one of his willing servants and ordered him to take care of the liquidation of the future heir. Disguised as a trustworthy monk the servant allured the little innocent boy to follow him and carried him off into the deserted forest and left him to his fate. With his “twelve pieces of silver” he went away and became a mercenary. For years he moved from one theater of operation to another; his guilty conscience, however, continued to press heavily on him. Becoming older he decided to return to his native land. There he confessed his sin to the prior of the convent of Reinhausen and pleaded to be admitted. The abbot, however, imposed on him to suffer the same fate as the young heir and ordered him to live deep in the forest far away from human beings. After an endless search the penitent sinner found a small cave underneath an overhang of a rock where he established his miserable “hermitage” that formerly had served as a dwelling for a tribe people of the past known as “Hurkut”.

When walking from the village and along the fringe and later through the forest in a northeasterly direction we arrived at a height, called “Mackenröder Spitze”. There stood a viewing tower, an open wood-beam construction, but protected by a roof. From its top one had a fantastic outlook, and on clear weather conditions the silhouettes of the "Harz" mountain range, the highest in Northern Germany, could be admired. Its highest point, once a volcano a million years ago, with an altitude of 1,140 m (3,420 ft) was now situated in Eastern Germany. The highly guarded border went right through the area of that mountain. From this viewing point you could climb down and follow the valley to a place called "Ebergötzen". In this village Wilhelm Busch, a famous painter and poet, who still has a place in the hearts of all Germans and is often quoted, was living in the second half of the 19th century. He is the original inventor of "comic books". His *Max and Moritz*, the forerunner of the *Katzenjammer Kids*, was translated into countless languages. Nearby this place was a circular lake, the "Seeburger See", where we later enjoyed boat rides. The impressive water source, "Rhumequelle", the greatest single source in Germany, was a bit too far for walking and was visited by bicycle, as well as "Osterode", a small town on the slopes of the Harz mountains. There we discovered a giant former storage complex for grain. It originated from the period when the Hanoverian prince elect became King George I of Great Britain and Hanover (personal union). From this impressive building, which still bears the English royal coat of arms over its front entrance, the miners of the mountain area were supplied with corn in times of famine. To the nearly "Sösetalsperre", a long stretched artificial lake in the mountains, we made our first long tour by bike and slept there overnight underneath the triangles-buttoned together former military awnings. There was a funny rumor that on certain Sundays one could listen to the tolling of the bells of the village church's steeple, which was submerged at the time when the barrage was constructed.

The only fairly well-conserved ruin of a fortified castle near our place was the "Plesse", close to the university city in a northerly direction. Further down in the valley on the "Pappelhof" resided a friend of my mother's, a respected local author, K. H.

Kurz. Unfortunately he was handicapped because as tank commander he had lost both of his legs in Russia, but he was quite agile in his wheel chair and could walk slowly when he strapped on his artificial wooden legs. He told me exciting stories about the knights, who used to live in those fortified "mountain nests", about their fighting for prerogatives and lands, their tournaments, socage service, torture chambers, dungeons and minnesingers (touring singers of the nobility). He told me of course something about the history of the "Plesse" up on the mountain. He explained to me that those high-positioned fortified places had always a problem with the water supply. The situation became intolerable, when in case of armed disputes and bigger war conflicts the whole population from the surrounding villages including their cattle fled into the "Burg" of their lord for protection. Some circumspect knights had taken precautions and built extremely deep wells employing prisoners and socage service to do the hard labor. The greatest impediment was the often massive rock. Explosives were still unknown at this time, but they found a clever solution. Wedges of dry wood with a high grade of absorption capacity were hammered into fissures and continuously soaked with water. By inserting always bigger and bigger wedges the rock finally gave in and cracked. It took an endless time to conquer the hard rock, but with perseverance and patience and sometimes years of drudgery the work finally was accomplished with a simple method copied from nature. The same method was used to get through the hard rock when constructing secret underground passages, a precaution for situations when the castle had to be sealed completely when it was besieged. In case of emergency provisions and information could be brought stealthily through these often kilometer-long passages by trustworthy but inconspicuous persons such as old women or those acting as such. Often these old passages were never used and were completely forgotten and sometimes only discovered later on by chance.

To give me a better idea of the past history K. H. Kurz gave me the novel *Ivanhoe* by Sir W. Scott, a world-famous story of a courageous knight in medieval England. That incited me to play knight for a time. I carved myself a sword and prepared a big shield that I decorated with a formidable curled-up snake.

Forester E. doted on me and I was welcome to accompany him when observing the red deer and wild boar, on the condition that I kept my mouth shut and sat motionless throughout our stay on the high stand. I could also participate at battues chasing wild boars in the direction of the hidden hunting party. He taught me shooting with a 6 mm sub-caliber rifle and later even with buckshot. After some training my shooting results were rather good. My only minor disadvantage was that I had to bring the gun to my left shoulder when taking aim because the sight of my right eye had suffered a bit after two surgical eye operations.

Our primitive home, Villa Mud, did not prevent friends and relatives from paying us a visit. To solve this problem we had an arrangement with the owner of the "Black Bear" where they could stay for the night or longer with rudimentary comfort. The innkeeper had in the meantime furnished a few guest rooms. For a time there was also resident a regular tenant, a former major of the army. My visiting grandfather made his acquaintance and was very happy to have found a partner with whom he could exchange views about historical and military subjects.

Another frequent visitor was Uncle "Ohm" Walther S., the brother of my grandma in the city. He was the same person we had met in Halle, and we had enjoyed his and his wife's hospitality on our escape from Silesia in January 1945. He was a retired professor of German philology and now a widower. He was a typical representative of those effulgent academics, who used to pontificate on everything in a lecturing manner, with Latin and French and sometimes even Greek expressions, and delivered endless sophisticated speeches about poets, thinkers and philosophers in the highly polished German of scholars hardly comprehensible to the mass of common citizens. He was an absolute theorist, who seemed never in his life to have cleaved firewood, used hammer and nail or washed his socks. His forte was his brilliant memory concerning intellectual matters. In his everyday life he was continuously in need of a "body guard", a person to take care of the trivial problems of the monotonous daily round. I remember one typical incident that demonstrates the situation: One pleasant summer evening we both took a walk together along the country road leading east. A woman with the typical head scarf of the villagers approached us with her handcart fully loaded with green fodder for her rabbits and goats, which she had cut with her sickle somewhere. When she came close "Ohm" Walther lifted his sturdy walking stick and pointed it toward the woman and lifted his other hand to indicate her to stop and shouted with his sonorous commanding voice: "Wait a moment my dear woman! Do you have the slightest idea, what you have got on your means of transport there?"

"Green fodder for my animals, gracious Sir!" the woman uttered finally extremely irritated. With a lifted shaking index finger he indicated that he was absolutely dissatisfied with her simple answer and started to lecture us in detail about the different types of grass, about clover, lupine, herbs and flowers designating them with their Latin and French names, their origins, properties and usefulness. Finally he discharged the speechless and flabbergasted woman to her animals and wished her a pleasant evening. One can imagine easily the stories that circulated around the community about the erudite crazy professor. I remember Uncle "Ohm" Walther as always being a bit depressed. Even years later he never managed to overcome the sad fact that his only son had been killed in action in France during the invasion of Normandy. His sister, my grandma, however, was not an easy woman to deal with and had a lot of arguments with him about his unpractical academic ways.

We had already been living for some time in our Villa Mud

(so called because of the steep muddy lane with deep ruts that passed our hut at the garden side) when suddenly and completely unexpected the former husband of our predecessor Mrs. H. appeared, released finally as a POW. Probably he had got the address from his mother. One can really imagine the disappointment and rage of the officer divorced in absentia on hearing the story of his former wife's shady new husband and her attitude. After the war there had been uncountable cases similar to this one where women had taken other husbands, even foreigners, soldiers of the occupying forces. My mother was feeling very sorry for him and tried to cheer him up. He stayed for a while and slept on a folding army camp bed. He did some farm work and put his personal documents in order at the authorities in the city. In the meantime his mother had moved to Goettingen. His brother had started a coal-trading business in a coastal city in Northern Germany and offered him a partnership. He left us but his mother stayed in Goettingen and my mother kept contact, paying her a visit from time to time. She was a very distinguished, educated and witty lady. She and my grandmother Hitta became good friends at first sight. Both spent hours with "Patience", a card game, telling the future from cards, reading and reciting poetry and talking about supernatural happenings. Her small living quarters looked like an oriental bazaar with many carpets, thick cushions and brass objects.

Another remarkable acquaintance of my mother was Graf H. After having been discharged from the American POW camp in the United States he did not have a leg to stand on, having been a professional officer with no other professional training. His close relatives had all perished in the war. He was a practical man and was lucky to meet a former subordinate from wartime, a well-meaning mechanic with a workshop in a suburb of Goettingen, who took him in as a partner and started to realize small technical ideas. Empty brass shells of artillery ammunition, for example, were transformed into oriental-looking beautifully chased

"Mocca coffee mills". Soon roasted coffee beans appeared again on the shelves of the provision merchants' and the mocca mills sold like hot cakes. They adapted to a new trend in the cities and started to produce the first primitive refrigerators for private households. Unfortunately we lost contact when he moved away.

General von H. was another noteworthy friend of ours. He lived in the nearby heavily bomb-damaged city of Kassel. He spent nearly a decade as a POW in a camp in Siberia/Russia and had survived coldness and starvation with iron discipline. He had immediately started to learn Russian and was highly esteemed by the Russian guards and their superiors. If there were any problems he was asked to intercede. In the POW camp he had introduced academic education courses in order to keep his fellow prisoners intellectually fit and to distract them from their pitiful situation. Previously the suicide rate had been high. The Russian POW camp commander had organized books and writing utensils.

A fellow prisoner who was a tailor in his civil profession taught him a lot about his trade, and he was later able to alter and even sew simple garments. Thanks to this dexterity in using thread and needle he was in a position to keep his head above water by getting some extra bread from time to time. He explained to us that people who were trained in a practical craft always had a better chance to survive critical situations than theorists. After his release, and he had settled down in the West (his family came also from the German Far East), he pledged all his three sons to learn a useful handicraft before they started to study at the university. He was a remarkable personality with an enormous sense of humor. I think the latter was also a reason that he survived the time in Russia while millions of POWs perished.

I already mentioned my uncle the "East African" and ethnologist. During his studies in Goettingen he was living in a small attic room above a butcher's shop near the railway station. The office of the dentist Dr. K. who took care of my teeth was not far away. I was already more independent and took every morning the newly introduced yellow mail bus to Goettingen to join the Buerger (school) for a better education. I had still experienced the installation of the successor to Schoolmaster B. in the village. My new school was situated near the street where my grandmother was living. In order to make it possible for me to join the city school I had to register as a city resident at her address. It was of course an illegal trick. I used to get my lunch at grandma's place and also prepared my homework there. At lunch I also often met a destitute nephew of my grandma whom she supported too. He also studied law like her daughter and had come from the Russian zone leaving everything behind. Most of the time I returned home by taking the evening bus.

One day I decided to pay my uncle Axel the "African" a visit and climbed the steep steps up to his student den. When I silently opened the door my surprise was great to see him nude together with a beautiful female fellow student also stark naked on his bed completely absorbed in "offering a sacrifice to Aphrodite". I was extremely sorry not to have been at his place; anyway for such kind of "penetrating" activities I was still very young. Unnoticed I closed the door silently and left the "lover's nest" and decided to adjourn my visit to another day. Later I accosted him, tactfully mentioning his activities with that ardent attractive young lady. He kept cool and explained to me, smiling, that what I had seen was the most suitable and pleasant occupation for people of his age. To avoid, however, inconvenient and unwelcome problems one had to choose the right moment. I did not dare to pose questions concerning his remark to not be exposed to ridicule and had to wait some time until the meaning of this council had been explained to me by somebody competent.

I was very proud when a postal savings book was opened for me. The times of the "Sparschwein" (money saving box in the form of a pig) were over. My grandmother took care about my earning some pocket money to fill the account. She was living on the third floor of a clinkered city house with no elevator. I was in charge to haul up firewood, coal, glasses with preserved food and dried laundry from the cellar. I also took care of shopping and other errands. When she went on a journey I assisted her carrying the luggage to the bus and railway station. In times of good weather when I had finished my homework we used to take a stroll over the "Wall", the former rampart of the city from medieval times that was still intact and enclosed the whole center of the old part of the town. In one of the houses leaning at the rampart Prince Bismarck, the German imperial chancellor, used to live, when he was a young student in Goettingen. My grandma told me that he had been arrested several times and jailed in the lock-up of the university for dueling with pistols and for other foolish student actions. The rampart was bordered like an alley with trees on both sides. When the lime trees were in blossom it smelled wonderful. Grandma always collected some blossoms for making tea. The wall was cut by streets leading into the center. On one of our strolls grandma treated me with my first ice cream in a waffle cone from a street vendor.

Of all my school subjects I valued most the English lessons. They started with pictures and subtitles with their meaning. The pronunciation of the words was rehearsed until the teacher was satisfied. After we had acquired a sufficient amount of vocabulary and a bit of grammar we started to form phrases and then short stories followed. That is the usual way to learn one's own and foreign languages properly all over the world. We even were taught some popular English songs like "My darling is over the ocean" or "This old man". Thanks to the qualified and skillful teacher and the good textbook we were soon in a position to write English essays. I was very proud about my good marks in English, but the greatest joy was when I could afford to buy an English dictionary in a book store and got my first English story book in the public library. I still remember its title; it was *Little*

Prince by Antoine de Saint Exupéry, a French pilot and famous author. International literature opened to me the gate to a completely new world. I felt like Aladdin who ordered the treasure chamber to open up with the magic formula "Open Sesame!" Our tutor in mathematics certainly knew his subject extremely well but unlike his English-teaching colleague was absolutely incapable to impart it. Disregarding one natural talent in our class the result was as one would expect: disastrous; all the rest got bad marks. The tutor was drifting in his academic clouds and should have better worked as a scientist alone behind the screens. He was a very nice person, so we felt very sorry for him. I admit that mathematics is not one of my strong points, but it is my absolute conviction that normal people can learn and comprehend everything if it is explained well and patiently. Some persons comprehend fast and others need just a bit longer. That does not mean of course that "you can teach a horse writing"!

In the center of our village on an elevated plot and at a street crossing, a strategically favorable spot, which all the villagers had to pass, lived a "crazy" person. Mrs. S. was staying together with her daughter and a disabled ex-soldier K. in a small half-timbered house. She was of an indefinable age. With her black habit and headscarf, the many gaps between her decayed teeth, her hooked nose and her bowed-down bearing she looked like the evil witch from the fairy tales and stirred our fantasy. Provocatively we youngsters often gathered at a safe distance from her little house and started to sing "Hänsel und Gretel gingen in den Wald ...!" (Jack and Jill went into the forest ...!). She was of course not specially amused about it and appeared with her birch broom to chase us away. She was the greatest chatterbox of the village. She insisted on knowing everything, and that, too, even better than others. She heard literally "das Gras wachsen!" (the growing of the grass; she fancied herself to be a know-it-all). Her glib tongue with the piercing voice never seemed to reach a halt. Nobody could match her loquacity. She spread the most thrilling rumors about people she did not even know and about matters she could not pass judgement on at all. Somehow she was peculiar – "a queer fish" – and the villagers poked fun at her behind her back. Finally she got a job in Goettingen and could no more waylay the passers-by and implicate them in an endless conversation. She was working as a seamstress in a factory for feather bedcovers. Quilts and feather bedcovers were articles in demand after years of frugality and improvisation, but were rather costly. Soon the crafty "rumor monger" discovered an additional source of income. She made a tour around the village and pestered the people to treat themselves with the luxury of a new quilt from the factory where she worked and where she had the privilege to get those fine articles for a reduced employee's price. Like all the other gullible people our frugal mother, who had not long ago used sewn-together flour sacks as bedsheets, was taken in and made a 50 percent down payment as requested. The scoundrel had fleeced everybody. The ordered items were never delivered and the money "went up the chimney". At that time we moved to the city and heard later that somebody had taken the initiative and notified the authorities about this case of mass fraud. The culprit was sentenced to a prison term, but the prepaid money was never seen again.

The exact opposite of this creature was the imposing older farmer W. He was an educated, open-minded personality and a highly respected member of the farmer's association. He was the "gray eminence" behind the scenes and the driving power for the modernizing of agriculture and new methods of cultivation, the introduction of better seed and new kinds of field plants when the bad times were over. As was to be expected he got a lot of resistance from the more-conservative fraction, but by demonstrating his ideas on his own lands he convinced most of them in the long run. He was lucky that his daughter chose the right husband. His son-in-law became a very successful farmer and his lands included in later years the areas of many neighboring communities, where he put into practice the innovations of his father-in-law, who received the highest civil order of the Federal Republic of Germany, the Distinguished Service Medal.

Another extreme case again was the "Lanz-Bulldog" tractor driver and farmhand R., who was working for farmer W. When he was sober, he was an easy-going person and a good worker, but as soon as he got near "the bottle", and that happened quite often, especially on payday at the end of the month as he was a drunkard, he lost his control and beat his wife to a jelly. When Pastor S. after having interfered on such an occasion asked her why she did not simply apply for a divorce, she told him that she had got so used to it that she did not mind anymore and probably would miss the rubdowns!

In the early fifties the mayor and the schoolmaster were informed that an official health control of the community, in particular, of the children, would soon take place. At the determined date a closed Red Cross truck accompanied by doctors, medics and nurses from the regional public health department appeared for the checkup and was parked in front of the school. First we got injections against poliomyelitis and something else; next we had to swallow some pills and were examined very closely like at an inspection by a military recruitment board. This was followed by a general information and counseling of the parents. All children were sent in groups into the schoolhouse and a medic explained some elementary rules of health to us. The teeth were not overlooked but checked by a dentist, toothbrushes were distributed free of charge and the most effective way of its use was explained meticulously and demonstrated. Today it might sound incredible, but there were a couple of children, who had never made the "acquaintance" with a toothbrush in their life to this very moment.

The frequent occurrence of certain given/first names of the

male village population was a striking fact. I am sure that the bearers of those names had never wasted a thought on where it originally derived from. In most of the cases they had simply taken over the names of their fathers, godfathers or forefathers. “Hermann” (Henry) was very popular after “Hermann/Arminius der Cherusker”, a Teutonic chieftain, who beat the army of the Roman viceroy of Germany Varus. “Karl” (Charles) came from the emperor Charlemagne the Great. “Wilhelm” (William) was the name of three of our former emperors in the 19th century; the latter, William II (“Kaiser Bill” for the English people), had been the grandson of queen Victoria. “Otto” had been the name of a famous German king and that of Prince von Bismarck, the chancellor of three emperors. “Friedrich” (Frederic) was of several historical personalities, that of Emperor Barbarossa (Redbeard), Frederic the Great, Prussian king and philosopher in the time of Voltaire and Catherine the Great of Russia and, last but not least, the short-lived emperor Frederic III, who was married to the eldest daughter of Queen Victoria. Very popular was the name Albert, probably after the respected German husband and Prince Consort of Queen Victoria, because I cannot find any other outstanding German historical figure of this name of the past. “Georg” (George) was the name of three British-Hanoverian rulers in the 18th century. So far I can remember there was absolutely no youngster born in the 1930s and 1940s with the name “Adolf”; it is rather strange, because the dictator had for a time been rather popular in Germany.

Contrary to the present day, quite a few different professions were represented in our village, even a blacksmith who took care of horseshoes and other objects of his trade, but one was missing, a regular gravedigger. This task was taken care of by some always-changing volunteers. In summer, when it was hot, the burials took place within a short time as a cool chapel for a longer “lying in state” did not exist. We were always feeling sorry for the men who were digging the pits in winter, when the ground was frozen and hard like stone. The winter season was much colder and longer at that time. At some funerals we were listening concealed from behind the hedge of the graveyard when Uncle Ernst, the pastor, made his memorial sermon, and we were amazed about the wonderful things that were promulgated about the deceased, who in their lifetime had often really not led an exemplary existence. Pastor S. took care that even the greatest sinner of the village got a decent departure.

Somewhere we had heard the rumor that cemeteries are places that were haunted at midnight. The ghosts of the deceased were supposed to wander aimlessly around with lights in their hands and clad in white, drifting tunics. One night I left our hut stealthily to meet as arranged a friend of mine in order to get on the track and find out the truth. Hidden in a tree we were on the lookout around midnight, but we were disappointed. Besides a crying owl, a cat chasing mice and some passing bats nothing happened. The only lights we saw were those of glowworms dancing over the graves. The owner of the "Black Bear" told us that one summer night a rolling drunk had lost his way and had somehow got into the cemetery near his home. There he had stumbled into a just-prepared pit and had overslept there in his drunken fit until the funeral party arrived next morning and he was resurrected.

There was another trade that was missing in the village, a barber and a ladies "coiffeur". There had been a "Figaro", but he had passed away and no successor had been in sight. Mum took care of our haircut, and she also managed to keep herself presentable,

She had simple curling tongs that had to be placed onto the embers of the oven before being applied. The womenfolk assisted each other before festivals and special occasions, when the usual head scarfs or old-fashioned hats and berets were put aside. According to this situation there were no great variations in the hair fashion. Men's and boys' hair were cut short; long hair like today and men with horsetails and similar styles did not exist yet. The girls often had pigtails or rather short open hair, and women had a bun or had tresses or curled them up at both sides. The less vain ones put their hair up with needles or kept it rather short. When shampoo was not available in all the difficult years one had to use simple curd soap as for the laundry. I went later to a reasonable student barber in the city. It was just 1 DM per treatment. Nowadays it is very expensive; we call that inflation. I remember exactly that one breakfast roll was just 0.06 DM (6 pennies).

As you might have already guessed, I have a distinct and sensible sense of smell and try to remember those typical ones of that period of my life.

There was the heavy smell of axle grease for the wagons and farm equipment. Everywhere the smell of the muck of the farm animals was prevailing. A huge dung heap was near the stables and sheds in the courtyard of the farmhouses. The manure was the only means of fertilizing at that time. A full cesspool was considered as a treasure and equal to a full bank account. The importunate pungent smell of ammonia in the horse stables was very different from the equally penetrating one of the poultry runs. On Saturdays the smell in the houses of soft soap and floor wax was overpowering, and at festival days it was still surpassed by the smell of mothballs from garments hung unused for a long time in the wardrobe or coming from the chests. There was a special room in about every farmhouse reserved for festivities to receive guests and official visitors. It was called "Die gute Stube" (the fine room) and it always smelled dusty and stifling because it was locked most of the time. Where many people came together it was smelling of healthy sweat. Contrary to the present day, when technic and electronic govern everything, people had to work hard from early morning to late in the evening, and the sanitary installations were still very primitive.

Another typical smell was that of freshly mown grass and the dried grain and the hay in the barn and loft. In springtime there was the fragrance of countless wild flowers, the blossoms of the fruit trees and the fresh smell of the sprouting leaves of the beech trees in the forests. Typical also was the overpowering fragrance of lilac that was growing near about every house. In autumn it was the smoke of the potato-top fires, that of the manure spread on the fields and that of the fermenting silage of fodder beet. In the public houses it was the odor of stale beer and heavy tobacco smoke. Even some people had their personal smell. The pastor and Uncle Hermann were always surrounded by an aura of heavy cigar smoke, and my mother as well as Hitta, my other grandmother, emitted the smell of the fresh "Eau de Cologne 4711" perfume until they could afford something better. My favorite smell in the starving years, however, was that of smoked sausages from the window of the curing room "Wurstekammer" of farmer H. and the aroma of still-hot bread in the bakery.

And what about the background sounds typical of the village? On the farms that had not been mechanized, computerized and specialized as in our present day, there existed countless different animals with their continuous concert. First at dawn or when it was often still dark, depending of the season there was the lowing of the cows reminding the farmer's wife that they wanted to be milked. At dawn it was followed by the polyphonic sound of the birds, the cooing of the pigeons, the crowing of the cocks, the cackle of their "harems", the clucking of the turkeys and the bleating of sheep and goats and, last but not least, the quacking of the geese and ducklings waddling to the pond. Next came the neighing of the teams of horses or the lowing of the oxen harnessed to coaches or wagons, the contented grunting and squeaking of pigs being fed, and there was the regular heavy-warning strike of the clock from the steeple of the church and on Sundays the tolling of the bells. The yelping of the many chained watchdogs was always present except in great heat or frost when they retreated into their kennels. Technical sounds were not many, just the starting sound of the Lanz-Bulldog the sturdy indestructible one-cylinder tractor from the 1930s, the metallic noise of moving farm equipment and the screeching of the circular wood saw cutting firewood. Such a potpourri of sounds can be very charming once you get used to it. Many of them are missing nowadays, but some have replaced them, they are all of a technical and electronic nature.

For a time there was just one working telephone in the community, that of Auntie Miele in the post office. Young people cannot believe it in a time where almost everybody seems to have a mobile phone.

If you drive through a village as a stranger it appears dull and uninteresting, but a village is like a kaleidoscope hidden in a wooden box. Once you open it and the light of the sun falls onto the multicolored glass fractions, it begins to glisten and to sparkle, and when you shake it, it gets even more fascinating.

My young days in that small unknown village were coming to an end. For educational reasons my mother had decided to move to a suburb of the university city. Lodging problems were still difficult and for that reason mum became a member of a building cooperative. She had to pay a regular membership subscription and obtained the right to be a tenant in a newly built house when it was her turn. The housing program was supported by the government, and families with children were given priority. Finally we got the long-expected notice and assembled our modest belongings and left our beloved Villa Mud that had been taken to our heart, in a horse-drawn box wagon that contained our furniture and a few other belongings. Notwithstanding our many limitations and the primitive conditions I had a wonderful and exiting time, great liberty during a disturbed time where every day signified a little step forward.

A whole nation and continent had been turned upside down and former enemies had become friends. People had met and mixed what otherwise never would have happened. Something good after all!

Many, especially older people, had gone off the rails or had acquiesced, but for others, first and foremost the young generation, the situation offered a completely new perspective and prospects for the future.

Today I consider myself a world citizen who prowled about the furthest corners of our globe. When I visualize the period of my youth I also have to think about the countless children and adults all over the world, who in consequence of wars, catastrophes and political conditions have lost their roots and have to build up a new existence far away from their native lands.